A DEATH AT STATION ALPHA

FROM THE MURDER ON MARS SERIES

By Greg Fowlkes

Includes a special preview of
THE BLOOD RED SANDS OF MARS
PART ONE FROM THE MURDER ON MARS SERIES

A DEATH AT STATION ALPHA

© 2012 The Fictional Press
www.TheFictionalPress.com

Published by The Fictional Press

The Fictional Press, an imprint of Intrepid Ink, LLC, provides full publishing services to authors of fiction and non-fiction books, eBooks and websites. From editing to formatting, to publishing, to marketing, Intrepid Ink gets your creative works into the hands of the people who want to read them.

Find out more at www.thefictionalpress.com.

ISBN 13: 978-1-937022-56-3

Printed in the United States of America

FOREWORD

The genesis of this novel lies in a question posed by my publisher shortly after the publication of *The Blood Red Sands of Mars* in which I was asked if I was planning a sequel. My response was that I had not been considering one, but of course I immediately began to hash over ideas in my mind. As I had been reading, at the time, a large numbers of mystery novels from the early twentieth century in my role as editor for Resurrected Press, my prospective plots ran in that vein. I decided that I would frame the new novel along the lines of a traditional English locked room mystery.

While a number of my previous works had employed the elements and the style of the mystery, notably the *Wizard at Law* fantasy series and the short novel *The Fictional Detective*, none of them is, strictly speaking, a true mystery or detective story. *The Blood Red Sands of Mars* is more of a science fiction action story or thriller than a mystery. And so, the concept that was to become *A Death at Station Alpha* was something of a departure for me, but I decided that the new work would follow the form of the "Golden Age" British mystery where the framing of and the solution to a puzzle is more important than the action.

I also quickly decided on using a variation of the English country house party as the setting of the plot. In this form, a limited number of loosely related characters are brought together in an isolated setting. One of their number is murdered, and the remaining characters are the only suspects. A detective or policeman is brought in from the outside and the solution is presented in the last chapter when all the suspects are gathered in the parlour. For a writer, this provides a rather neat package with few extraneous details to worry about. I merely transposed the setting from a country estate to an isolated research station on Mars.

The fact that almost thirty five years had passed since I wrote the initial draft of *The Blood Red Sands* posed certain difficulties. That novel was written shortly after the *Viking* landers and was more or less based on what was known about Mars at the time. *A Death at Station Alpha* was written post *Spirit* and *Opportunity* and all that thirty five years of remote exploration has discovered about the red planet. This obviously results in some issues of continuity. I largely decided to ignore the problem and base my Mars on that described in the original novel with a few changes that seemed appropriate. As the story is more about the people than the science, this seems a reasonable approach.

A Death at Station Alpha takes place roughly three years after the first book. Mars is a little more settled and civilized, though most of the planet is still unexplored and unoccupied. Inspector McKernan is still the central character, though I have introduced a new character, Constable Ortiz, because, frankly, every detective needs a foil if only to say "Elementary, my dear Ortiz," to.

At several points during the novel there are references to "The Morrison Case." For those readers interested in the details, I refer them to The Blood Red Sands of Mars, which is the account of that case.

My usual method of writing is very linear. I begin with an opening scene and write more or less straight through in order until I reach the conclusion. This works well for the average action story, and has the advantage of keeping the writer interested as he waits to see how it will all work out.

However, this approach is more problematic for a mystery. I know that there are some authors that have everything plotted out and detailed before they write the first word. I did start with the concept, a murder committed in a locked room (an airlock in this case) and an initial scene (card players at a remote research facility playing pinochle while a dust storm rages outside.) I had not, at the point where I typed the first scene, decided upon who was the murderer and how had they penetrated the locked room to perpetrate the crime.

I wrote the first few chapters hoping that an inspiration would come to me. Initially I was going to do something that owes more to Carolyn Wells than Agatha Christie, essentially involving the equivalent of a secret passage, but I junked that approach as "cheating." Fortunately, I had an epiphany of sorts that allowed me to "play fair" with the reader in which all of the necessary information is laid out from the beginning. I quickly wrote the last few chapters at this point, and then filled in the middle, hopping back and forth between chapters as the whim struck me. Occasionally, I needed to go back and rewrite some of the already completed chapters, but this usually only involved a few sentences or changing a time by a few minutes.

In the end, I think the process worked out fairly well. I believe that the solution to the puzzle is reasonable, but not too obvious, that I "played fair" with the reader by not concealing anything of importance, and that I did not resort to any special knowledge or abilities on the part of my detective. I do admit to breaking one of the rules of detective fiction, as formulated by the Detection Club, by introducing a Chinaman, though technically he is a sixth generation Chinese-American and the fact that he is of Chinese descent has no bearing on the mystery whatsoever.

As to the unasked question, yes, I am considering ideas for plots to a third Inspector McKernan mystery to complete the "Murder on Mars" trilogy. But that is for a later date. As for the present, I hope you enjoy *A Death at Station Alpha*.

Greg Fowlkes
July 12, 2012

Prologue
Day 0, 24:00-24:30

The four men were playing cards as they had every night for the last ten days. One of the periodic planet wide Martian dust storms had been raging and there was little else they could do. It was station policy that no expeditions were allowed outside during periods of reduced visibility. It was a sensible policy. Outside you couldn't see more than a dozen meters. There was little else for the scientists at Station Alpha to do but sleep, eat, work on reports—or play cards for hours on end.

They sat at a round table in the recreation room of the station. The only light in the room was the one above the table. Because of the storm, steps were being taken to conserve power, so only necessary lighting was on. The station had a small reactor, but relied on solar panels to supplement that. The dust blocked the light and got on the panels reducing their output. They'd have to wait until the storm was over and they could go outside to clean them off before things got back to normal.

They were playing pinochle. It was a game they were all pretty good at. They were also good at bridge, poker, euchre. They'd had lots of time to practice. They kept score, but weren't playing for money. It wouldn't have mattered much, anyway. None of them was that much better than the others for it to make a difference.

An alarm chimed over the airlock leading to the laboratory building, causing the card player facing that direction to look up. An older man came through the lock hatch, shutting it behind him which silenced the alarm. He walked up the hall towards the table. The recreation hall was in the station's administration building at the center of the complex. On either side of the administration building were dormitory wings connected to the main building by tunnels. The labs and workshops were in a building at right angles to that line making a "T" shape. You couldn't get from one building to another without going through the recreation hall.

"What's up, boss?" Daniel Chen, one of the card players called. "Any change in the weather?"

"Good news, boys," William MacKensie said. "I just got the latest met report. It looks like the dust will be dying down in a day or two and you'll be able to get back to work."

"It's about time," one of the other card players said. "I'm going stir crazy."

There was more on his mind than that. The chance to do field work on Mars was the opportunity of a lifetime for a young researcher. A successful season could make a scientists career, but if they couldn't gather enough information for a set of good papers they might as well forget it. They'd never get another chance to come out to Mars.

"Don't stay up too late," the station chief said as he headed through the air lock leading to the men's dormitory.

The card players called good night as he passed out of the room. Dr. William MacKensie was well liked. He was the grand old man of Martian geology. He'd been on the planet off and on for more than twenty five years and could have had his pick of positions at any of the best universities on Earth. Instead, he had chosen to remain on Mars doing what he liked best, fieldwork. He ran the station loosely, but didn't have much tolerance for sloppiness.

They resumed the card game. The clock on the wall showed "24:00," forty minutes to midnight. The Martian day was that much longer than Earth's. By convention, the length of hours and minutes were the same as on Earth. The difference was made up in the time between 24:00 and 00:00 with clocks rolling over at 24:40. All of the clocks on Mars were digital, driven by computers. The only one with hands was the one behind the bar at Finnegan's in Mars City which Finnegan himself reset every morning before opening up.

Another man came through the recreation hall in the direction opposite to that taken by MacKensie. It was Dr. Augustyn, the current number two man at the station. He was well known on Earth. The rumor was that he would be taking over as the head of the Planetary Institute next year.

"It's late," he chided as he passed the table. "You should all get to bed. You've got work to do, and you've all been slacking off during the storm. And turn out that light when you go. You're wasting power."

He didn't bother to wait for a response before taking the tunnel to the lab building.

"What a prick," commented one of the players. "Where does he get off?"

"He is second in command," Chen replied.

"Why does Mac put up with him?"

"Connections on Earth. He's brought in plenty of grant money."

"I don't know why. I've read his bloody papers. Not an original idea in the lot as far as I could see."

"Well he is right, it is getting late. And I'm getting bloody tired of pinochle."

"Let's at least finish the game. We don't want Augie to have the satisfaction of thinking he can boss us around.

CHAPTER 1
DAY 1, 08:15 – 09:00

McKernan's phone woke him. Outside, the wind was still throwing dust against the side of his hut. The storm had been blowing for over a week, blanketing the planet with a cloud of dust that wrapped all the way around Mars. It had everyone's nerves on edge including his own.

He glanced at the clock. It said 08:15. Sometimes he regretted the fact that phone coverage had been extended to this part of Hut Town. He had hoped to sleep in late. Ferris had had the duty shift the previous night, but when trouble broke out at Thelma's, McKernan had provided backup. It hadn't been a big deal, no serious injuries and not much damage, but by the time they'd put the last of the participants in the drunk tank it had been after 01:00.

He fumbled for the phone. The I.D. of the caller read "Hugo Garcia-Gomez." Garcia-Gomez was the interim Trust Authority Governor. It was never good when he called. Especially at 08:15.

"McKernan here," he answered.

"Erik. This is Hugo Gomez. There's been a death at Station Alpha."

Station Alpha was a research base some 1200 kilometers to the west. It was a regulation that all deaths on Mars were to be reported to the police. It wasn't usually the Governor that reported them, though.

"Is there anything suspicious about it?" McKernan asked.

"No, nothing suspicious. It's pretty clear. The dead man was found with a geologist's hammer embedded in his head." Gomez could have a strange sense of humor at times. His position was a curious one. Three years earlier the U.N. had promised Mars some form of limited self government, but in the manner typical of international organizations they were still hashing out the details. That had left the administration of the planet in the hands of a string of temporary governors.

McKernan's own position was just as ambiguous. Technically, he was still on his second three year contract with the Trust Authority, just another hired civil servant. He also had the support, or at least the acceptance of most of the old Mars hands. But after he had solved the Morrison murder Eric's profile had risen with the Trust Authority. He wasn't sure that that was a good thing.

"So it wasn't an accident or suicide?"

"No. I think that's pretty clear. The dead man is Dr. Augustyn, the number two at Alpha. He was a big man back on Earth, Eric. He was in line for taking over as the head of the Planetary Institute in the fall. His death is going to make waves. We need to be on top of this."

Gomez was a politician. He liked things to run smoothly. It made his life easier at budget appropriations time. The Trust Authority was run under U.N. auspices, and its funding depended on how much of a cut of the mining royalties the Trust Committee on Earth decided to give it. Gomez, like any good bureaucrat, wanted to get as big a cut as possible. His reasoning, which was probably accurate, was that the way to do that was to avoid waves. Keep the Corporations happy; keep the U.N. happy; keep Gomez happy. Besides, his appointment to Mars would be over in less than a year, and then it would be back to Earth for Garcia-Gomez.

"I want you to get out there as soon as possible and clear this mess up."

"Does that mean they don't know who did it?"

"No. There are only twelve people at Alpha at the moment, not counting the dead man. With this weather, no one else is probably any closer than Junction 3. Obviously, one of the people at Station Alpha is the murderer. You need to find out who, and do it fast."

"O.K. I'll get out there as soon as I can arrange a flight."

"That won't work. Everything is grounded because of this damned dust storm. You'll have to take ground transportation. "

"Great," McKernan thought. Station Alpha was fifteen hundred kilometers by what passed for roads on Mars.

"I've made arrangements for you to take the road train to Junction 3. It was supposed to leave at 08:00 this morning, but they are holding it for you. From there, you can pick up the local constable and take a buggy to Alpha."

Junction 3 was a thousand kilometers down the Mars road. At fifty kph. It would take at least twenty hours to get to Junction 3. From there it was another five hundred to Station Alpha, but the road was more of a track. It would probably take the better part of another day. He tried to remember the name of the constable on duty at Junction 3. He couldn't.

"Eric? Are you still there?"

"Yeah, I was just thinking."

"You can do your thinking on the road train. I had to pull strings to get them to wait for you. Get your kit together and get going."

"I should be on the road in less than an hour."

"Fine. Remember, Eric, it's important that this is cleared up quickly and neatly. Let me know when you get to Alpha."

Gomez hung up.

McKernan looked around his hut. It didn't look like much, but by Mars standards it was fairly luxurious. Fifty square meters of space all to himself. One end was given over to the plants he grew for oxygen and food. He'd upgraded the heater and even had a three burner cooking unit, not that he had much time to cook. He'd cobbled together a set of furniture from stuff he had scrounged over the six years he'd been on Mars. Not elegant, maybe, but comfortable. He'd added insulation and some extra shielding on the roof. He even had an old solar panel which he used to charge batteries.

The best part was that he had a chance to buy the hut next door from a mechanic who'd gotten a job on the other side of the planet. His place was in pretty good condition. If he put in a bulkhead door between the two, he'd have another fifty square meters of space. He'd be able to use one hut as living room/kitchen and the other as a bedroom/bath. The other hut even had a "back door," an airlock to the outside. In his line of work you never knew when that might come in handy. Of course, buying the other hut would take most of the cash he'd saved up. It would only make sense if he signed up for another three year contract when the current one ran out. He wasn't sure he was ready to do that.

Living space was at a premium on Mars where nearly everything had to be imported from Earth. Hut Town, was the cobbled together remnant of the original Mars base where those who weren't employed directly by the Trust Authority or one of the mining corporations lived. McKernan's position as head of the Trust Authority Police would have entitled him to a small single in the Authority's dorm block, but he preferred to live on his own. In the long run it was cheaper, roomier, and a lot more private. Having grown up in the L.A. barrios he valued the latter. Besides, living in Hut Town gave him a certain amount of perspective.

Funny, he thought, that somehow in the last three years Hut Town had become capitalized. In the six years he'd been on Mars he'd seen a number of changes, mostly for the better. It was still a pretty rough and wild place, but there were more people thinking of it as home. He was starting to think that he might be one of them.

He always kept a bag packed in case he had to travel in a hurry. Besides, he didn't have any place else to put the stuff. He checked it over to make sure he had what he needed. In addition to a couple of changes of underwear and another set of clothes, it had a small forensics kit and a camera. He'd be able to take finger prints and DNA samples, though getting the latter analyzed might take months. There was also an extra pistol and a knife concealed in a hidden compartment. He hadn't had to use either in over a year, but on Mars you always planned for the worst. If you didn't, you ended up dead.

He dressed in his usual uniform of jeans and sweater. There was another knife strapped to his leg and a small pistol in a shoulder holster. The latter was for use only as a last resort. With Mars buildings pressurized you didn't want to blow any holes in the envelope if you didn't have to. That's why the pistol was only a 6 mm. On Mars a lack of penetrating power was a good thing in a gun.

Satisfied with his packing, he grabbed the bag and another that held his surface suit and headed out through the front airlock into the corridor beyond. He activated the locking mechanism on the outside airlock door. It was an old fashioned manual combination lock, more reliable and harder to hack. Gaeretts, one of the local constables, had the combination so he could check up on his plants while he was gone.

It was cold in the corridor, but not as bad as some parts of Hut Town. This was one of the better parts, and the corridor's residents committee kept up the lighting and kept out the riff-raff. They'd even chipped in together to add a couple of centimeters of insulation. Parts of Mars City were almost getting cozy.

He walked down a couple of hundred meters of corridor and through a couple of airlocks until he got to the entry to the real Mars City, the part that was built of silica blocks and cement; where the temperature was a comfortable twenty degrees C., and the Authority was responsible for maintenance. This part was buried under sand to provide insulation and shielding and looked more like a shopping mall than a frontier.

The road train terminal was at the other end of a long hall, the largest indoor space on Mars. There was a small office and waiting room. The woman behind the counter recognized him. Most people in Mars City did.

"It's about time. The train was supposed to leave an hour ago. It's going to be hard to make up time with the dust storm."

"Sorry. This wasn't my idea."

"Yeah, I'm sure. It's Gate 1." There were no other gates. The road train was a fairly recent innovation. So was the road. It wasn't so much a paved road, as a path that had been plowed. The rocks had been pushed to the sides and any big pot holes had been filled. They'd extended it for a few thousand kilometers in either direction. The grand plan was to circle the planet, but that was years away. Still, it was the cheapest and most reliable route on Mars.

Gate 1 was an airlock at the end of a corridor. The airlock was open and the cabin of the road train's passenger compartment was on the other side.

"Been waitin'," the co-driver standing at the lock said. He slammed the gate and the road train's airlocks shut as soon as he was through.

He grabbed a microphone at the side of the airlock and talked to the cockpit, "He's aboard. We're buttoned up and ready to go." To Mckernan he said, "grab a seat."

McKernan had just enough time to drop into one of the empty seats before the road train shuddered into motion.

CHAPTER 2
DAY 1, 09:00 – 14:30

The road train consisted of a chain of three cylindrical cars, each about ten meters long and supported by a pair of large balloon tires at the front and back of each car. The first car was for passengers and crew, the middle for cargo that required pressurization, and the third was for unpressurized cargo. Sections of the roof on the third car could be removed to accommodate tall items. Each of the cars was powered by a gas turbine generator and carried its own supply of methane and oxidizer, but was controlled from the cab of the front car. On a good surface, the train could hit more than sixty kilometers an hour. The turning radius was a few hundred meters. Backing up was to be avoided if at all possible.

The passenger compartment of the first car resembled nothing so much as a the cabin of a commuter plane of the twentieth century. There was a row of five seats along each side with an overhead bin for luggage. The center aisle had just enough headroom for one to stand upright if you weren't too tall. The drivers' cab was at the front behind a thin partition. An airlock, life support and a small toilet compartment were at the rear. A row of small windows, one for each seat, was placed just too low for it to be convenient to see out of. The seats themselves consisted of a light metal frame with a mesh fabric seat and back. They weren't terribly comfortable, especially as the passengers would be in them for hours.

As McKernan had taken his seat at the rear of the car he had checked out the other five passengers. The two up front looked like technical or administrative types from one of the mining camps. Two others looked like they were miners at one of those camps heading back from r&r at Mars City. Most of the companies tried to make life at the camps bearable, but they also accepted the fact that an occasional trip to see fresh faces was good for morale. McKernan figured the remaining passenger for a prospector, one of the independent contractors that roamed the surface of Mars looking for a claim they could sell to the companies. You could make a fortune if you hit pay-dirt, but most just got by. Many died, victim to one of the many faces of death on Mars.

The road itself was about twenty meters wide. It had been graded flat, the rocks and boulders pushed to the side, and pot holes and depressions filled. It ran straight east-west except where the terrain prevented it. Any turns, with the road trains in mind, were gentle and the grade was kept to under ten degrees if possible. There were markers placed on either side of the road every hundred meters with every tenth marker numbered to indicate kilometers. Traffic was supposed to stay to the right, but as there wasn't any traffic that was more of a guideline than a rule. Under normal conditions, a road train could average better than fifty kilometers an hour.

From Mars City the road ran nearly two thousand kilometers to the west and about fifteen hundred to the east. There was talk of a north-south road being built, but that didn't look like it would happen any time soon. Spaced at irregular intervals of three to five hundred kilometers were turn offs to major corporate mining sites. Those roads were maintained by the companies and weren't nearly as grand as "the road." At each of these intersections a rest stop had been constructed. They were grandly called "Junctions" and numbered in order.

Near Mars City the road was in especially good condition, and McKernan noted that the driver seemed to be trying to make up for lost time. That was fine with him. It would be twenty hours to Junction 3 as it was.

There wasn't much to see out the window, just Mars, which tended after a while to a certain reddish brown sameness. McKernan was wide awake now, and despite the relatively flat roadbed, the road train tended to bounce around in the low gravity making sleep difficult. He might change his mind later, but for the moment he wouldn't even try to get some rest.

Instead, he pulled out his tablet to review the information he had downloaded on Station Alpha and its occupants. The station itself had been created about four years earlier as one of a projected set of permanent research stations to be built near particularly interesting locations. So far it was the only one in operation which was rather typical of the way things worked on Mars, McKernan thought.

Though it could handle fifty occupants at peak, Martian winter was setting in and it was down to eleven scientists and two support staff, a cook and a maintenance engineer. Make that ten live and one deceased scientist. The scientists were associated with some of the best research universities on earth. They would have to be. It was still expensive to send people to Mars, a round trip fare was more than most people made in a year, so only the best and the brightest, or the richest, made the trip.

The head of the station was Dr. William MacKensie. McKernan had met him a few times. He was one of the grand old men of Mars and had been on the First Martian Science Expedition twenty-five years earlier. He had spent much of the intervening time on Mars and probably had seen more of the planet than anyone. He certainly knew more about its geology than anyone else. From what McKernan remembered of him he was a likeable, straightforward man so confident in his own abilities that he didn't feel the need to emphasize his status.

The murdered man had been the station's number two, Dr. James Augustyn. This was his third stint on Mars, though he had been on planet a lot less than MacKensie, a total of about a two and a half years spaced out over the last fifteen years. He was currently the head of the geology department at the University of New South Wales, though one of the press clippings seemed to indicate that he as in line for something much grander. His list of publications was extensive, though McKernan noted that for the last ten years he was listed as senior rather than primary contributor. Like MacKensie, he was listed as single, though in Augustyn's case he was divorced, twice it appeared.

The remaining scientists were all operating on various national or private research grants and had no formal role in the administration of the station. They were:

Sigrid Oddsdottir – a native Icelander, she was the head of the department of geology at the University of Edmonton where she was currently on sabbatical. Forty-seven years old, she had been on Mars twice before. She was an expert on frozen soils.

Nils Jensen – Danish, 52, University of Aarhus, expert on the geology of Greenland, frozen soils and glaciers. Third time on Mars

Roger Morand – Australian, University of Sydney, 38, expert on cold weather volcanoes. Second time on Mars. Nickname "Breaker."

Boris Federenkov – Russian, 35, University of St. Petersburg, first time on Mars. Judging from the number of journal citations in his record he was an up and coming geologist

Sarah Toranaga – American, 32, USC, geologist, first time on Mars. Judging from the pictures in her file she was pretty hot. That might be motive enough on Mars.

The next four on the list were all young researches doing their first stint on Mars. There wasn't much information about any of them except their nationality, institution, scientific specialty, and list of publications.

David Chen – American, Arizona State, seismology

Antonio Berlanescu – Italian, University of Padua, geophysics

Dieter Frederichson – German, Max Plank Institute, stratigraphy

Sean Moran – Irish, University of Sydney, soil weathering

None of that pointed any one out as a likely murderer.

Jason Philips – maintenance engineer. He had been on Mars for four years, originally on a contract for United Semiconductor, but had taken the post at Station Alpha when that company had lost its concession in the aftermath of the Morrison case.

Molly MacDougal – cook and housekeeper. She had been on Mars for eight years. She had originally come out with her husband who had been a pilot. She was a trained nurse, so that wasn't that unusual with some of the mining companies, the idea being that husband-wife teams were more stable. At least that was the theory. Her husband had died in a plane crash a little over four years ago, but she had decided to stay on.

McKernan knew the last person on the list, or at least her husband. He had worked for Anglo-Martian Mining and had been the best pilot on Mars. It had been MacDougal who had checked McKernan out in the special planes used on Mars when he had first come to Mars six years ago. He had died in a crash flying during conditions when nothing should have been aloft. The rumor was that some executive with a lot of clout had demanded that he pick his party up at a remote mining camp so that he could make his connection back to Earth. MacDougal had crashed on the flight out to the camp.

There wasn't anything in any of the files that indicated a motive. He'd have to wait until he could interview the people at the base. The kilometer marker showed that they were still three hours from Junction 1.

Junction 1, when it came, was underwhelming, a cluster of huts on either side of the road. They were buried in the sand for protection against radiation so that only   the airlocks were exposed. A radio mast and a couple of dish antennas protruded from the biggest of the huts. A spur trail that McKernan knew led off towards Anglo-Martian's Number Two mine headed off to the north. The landscape was boring, a sand and boulder strewn plain with the low rim of a crater off in the distance. It was a little after local noon. The road train had been traveling for just over five hours.

The train stopped in front of the biggest of the huts. Someone came out of the hut and hooked a large flexible tube up to the airlock of the passenger car.

One of the drivers came out of the cab and announced in a bored voice, "We're going to be stopped for a half hour or so. I suggest you head in to the station. They've got water and food inside. If you need to use the facilities, you should do it here. They work better than the head on the train."

All six of the passengers including McKernan took the advice. After five hours he felt the need to stretch his legs.

The interior of the hut was as Spartan as the exterior. The airlock at the hut end of the tube disgorged them into a large room about twenty meters long and a ten wide. There were some benches along each side and a counter at the far end. Piled on the counter next to a spigot were some plastic cups and a pile of ration bars which seemed to be all the amenities Junction 1 had to offer. A sign said "water $1, food $5." There was a jar to put money in and a credit card reader. McKernan wasn't surprised when his fellow passengers swiped their cards for everything they took. Martians tended to be honest. They never knew when their lives might depend on the person next to them. Also, he suspected they were using company credit cards.

The water was flat and tepid. The ration bars, which were a local product made of various chopped vegetables were surprisingly good. None of the passengers seemed to be in a particularly talkative mood, and when the driver announced it was time to reboard, they all filed through the tunnel to the train.

The attendant came out to uncouple the tube and they started off again. Junction 2 was eight hours away. McKernan thought to himself that he'd better try and get some sleep despite the bumpy ride.

CHAPTER 3
DAY 1, 14:30 – DAY 2 – 18:00

Junction 2 was little more than a wide spot on the road with a couple of huts on either side. McKernan had slept most of the eight hours the road train had spent to reach it. The only thing notable about their stop was that the station served a decent vegetable soup. An hour after they had stopped the familiar call to reboard the train came. The two miners stayed behind, waiting to hitch a ride up the side road back to their camp. It was now the middle of the Martian night and McKernan had little trouble falling back to sleep.

It was 07:00 the next morning when the train reached the junction. Junction 3 was the oldest and most substantial of the stations. Three tracks met there, two from mining camps and the one from Station Alpha, and an addition had been added to the waiting room hut that offered sleeping accommodations for people waiting for connections. Another hut on the other side had been outfitted as a restaurant and bar. It wasn't anything fancy, but with Mars City a day's travel away even by road train, Junction 3 served as a supply depot and meeting place for the independent prospectors in the vicinity. The couple that had the concession for the station had taken advantage of their situation and started a farm to provide fresh produce to the area. Given transportation costs and limitations, even the corporate mining camps took some of their crop.

McKernan was the last one off the train. As he entered the waiting room, a short, stocky Hispanic woman in a police uniform greeted him, "Inspector McKernan? Constable Ortiz." He took the offered hand and shook it. The grip was firm. Ortiz might be short, but there was a lot of muscle in her compact body.

McKernan knew that he had met her when she had first arrived on Mars about an Earth year ago, but he couldn't really remember her. The Trust Authority was responsible for staffing and he really didn't have much say in the matter. With plenty of candidates, the selection process was pretty rigorous, and so far he hadn't had any complaints. With less than two dozen constables to cover a planet with a land area nearly equal to Earth's, he had been glad of any help the Trust Authority saw fit to supply. Given the situation, Ortiz had been assigned the new post at Junction 3 almost immediately upon arrival. His only contact had been the weekly reports she filed, and he let his chief deputy Gaeretts handle most of the paper work.

"Constable, thanks for meeting me," McKernan said in way of acknowledgement. "Are we ready to go?"

"I thought you might like some breakfast, first, sir. I know that there's not much in the way of food on the train. The food here is actually pretty good. My buggy is ready to go as soon as we're done."

"That sounds like an excellent idea. Lead the way."

They moved into the dining room in the next hut and took a table. Unlike the other stations, some attempt had been made to make Junction 3's a little less stark and utilitarian. A number of pictures had been hung from the plastic walls. They were all of slight, tough looking men, some in surface suits posed against Mars buggy's and shelter huts, or the interior of the station. McKernan recognized some of them, had buried two. They were all independent prospectors or other more or less permanent

Martians. He noted that there was a fairly recent one of Ortiz.

They didn't have to wait long before a woman came out with two plates of food. She was in her late thirties, with short blonde hair with a touch of gray and she moved with economical gliding steps that only someone who's spent a long time on Mars uses. Ortiz greeted her, "Morning, Jenny. This is Chief Inspector McKernan."

"Nice to meet you, Inspector. You don't get out this way much. Morrison was a friend of ours. I'm glad you got the men who killed him."

Morrison was a prospector that had been murdered three years ago over a mining claim. It had been more than just claim jumping, though, and one of the corporations had lost their concession on Mars over the affair. The former Trust Authority Governor had been forced to resign, as well. The old timers on Mars were a close knit bunch and remembered things like that.

"Nice to meet you, too, Jenny, and if that food's as good as it smells, I might have to drop in more often." It wasn't an idle compliment. Breakfast consisted of scrambled eggs with onions and peppers with a side of fried potatoes and a couple of small circles of what looked like Canadian bacon. A small glass of what looked like tomato juice accompanied it. McKernan noted that the other diners in the room were being served the same.

The food was as good as it looked, and McKernan dug in. Other than salt, seasonings were in short supply on Mars, but the cook, who he assumed was Jenny, had found some herbs to give the eggs real flavor. The tomato juice was actually a peppery vegetable juice. What looked like Canadian bacon really was Canadian bacon and not some sort of soy substitute.

"Jenny and her husband grow all their own food here, they even raise chickens and a couple of pigs," Ortiz said. McKernan detected a note of pride in her voice. "She must be impressed by you, not everyone gets the bacon. There's not that much of it."

"Tell Jenny I'm honored." McKernan continued eating his meal. "Have you had much contact with the staff out at Station Alpha?"

"They don't really come in here much. It's nearly a day in and a day back for them. The maintenance guy, Philips drives in if there are supplies to pick up and usually brings one of the younger scientists for company. He's a quiet type, doesn't say much. They do their business, stay for dinner, sleep over and then drive back the next day. I've never really had much reason to talk to him. I've only been out to Alpha a couple of times, and that was just to familiarize myself with the road. You think one of them did it?"

"Who else? Was there anyone else within a few hundred kilometers?"

"Not that I know of. I keep tabs on all the prospectors in the area and I'm pretty sure none of them were working within a five or six hour drive. Particularly with the storm going on. Everyone's been hunkered down until yesterday when it started to lift."

"So it was one of the remaining twelve people at the station that did it. Not much more we can do until we get there and start poking around. I'm ready if you are," McKernan said pushing his chair back from the table.

The police station, in typical Martian fashion was quartered in a hut that connected to the far side of the hut housing the restaurant. A standard sized building thirty meters long and ten wide, it held a small office, a holding cell and sleeping quarters for the single constable posted to Junction 3. Airlocks at each end gave access to the surface.

"The buggy is parked out back. We'll have to put on our surface suits to get to it."

McKernan had expected the arrangement and was already pulling his suit out of the pack that he carried. Essentially a light weight space suit designed for the slightly more benign conditions on Mars, it consisted of a coverall, a helmet and a backpack containing an air tank, batteries, and air purification equipment. Because the atmospheric pressure on Mars was higher than the vacuum of space, surface suits were lighter weight and more flexible than deep space suits. With additional air tanks, the wearer could survive several days safely if not in comfort. McKernan dressed in his with sure practiced motions. He was pleased to see that Ortiz was just as efficient as she pulled on the suit that she had grabbed from the locker next to the rear airlock.

The airlock was just big enough to allow the two of them to cycle through together. Outside, the mars buggy was waiting for them, a short cylinder suspended between four balloon tires, essentially a smaller version of the passenger car of the road train except that it was powered by a hydrogen fuel cell. The pressurized compartment could support two people for a week or more. With a trailer to carry additional supplies, some prospectors would go out for a month.

The airlock on the buggy would only pass one person at a time. McKernan let Ortiz go first so she could start the warm up. By the time he had cycled through the lock and popped the helmet of his suit she had already fired up the turbine and was running through the checklist. The inspector took the seat next to the constable and watched her work through the list without comment.

As soon as he was belted in, Ortiz eased the buggy out around the side of the hut to the road out front. A short distance down the road she turned into a side track heading to the north.

"Station Alpha is about four hundred and seventy kilometers. It should take us about ten hours if we don't run into problems."

"You expecting any?"

"Not unless the storm piled up some sand somewhere," Ortiz answered, concentrating on her driving. The track was not nearly as well prepared as the road. A path scarcely wider than the buggy, it had been plowed and leveled, but not much more. If two vehicles met at any of the tight spots, one of them would have to back up until there was enough space to pass.

The terrain rapidly became more rugged than the relatively flat plain on which the road was situated. The route had been chosen for the straightest line practical rather than to allow consistently higher speeds as the road had. At times they slowed to twenty kph climbing over ridges before picking up to fifty or more on the flats. Ortiz knew what she was doing, and drove with few wasted motions.

Three quarters of an hour or so into the drive they had reached a relatively flat plateau and the trip settled into a steady rhythm.

"How'd you end up on Mars, Ortiz?" McKernan asked to break the boredom.

"Usual story. I grew up poor in Brownsville Texas. I enlisted in the Air Force straight out of high school. I thought I'd learn a marketable skill like mechanic or computer technician, or even a cook. They put me in the Air Police. When my six year hitch was up I decided I liked being a cop, but not being in the military, so I didn't re-up.

But you know how things are on Earth, ten people applying for every decent job. I wasn't having much luck until I saw a job listing for the U. N. Trust Authority for an opening on Mars. I applied. I'd served a year as security at Moon Base, so I was already space rated. Six weeks later I was on a ship headed to Mars."

McKernan smiled. Ortiz's story wasn't that different than his own, a stint in the military flying jets and helicopters in Burma, studying law on the G.I. bill, no job prospects until the offer from the Trust Authority to head up the then almost non-existent police force.

"How do you like it, so far?"

"It's not bad, I guess. Mostly boring. Every week I do a patrol of the road from Junction 3 to End of the Line and back to check on conditions. Keep my ear to the radio in case I have to rescue anyone out on the surface. Not much real police work. The occasional prospector coming in and getting a little too drunk or rowdy, but Junction 3 is pretty tame that way compared to Mars City from what I hear. Most of the prospectors around here are older and wiser, and Jenny and her husband keep a pretty firm hand on things. Did have a guy who was breaking into prospector huts and stealing stuff. Lucky I caught him before some of the prospectors did. He'd have found himself out on the surface without a suit. That's about the extent of the crime I've dealt with."

"So you've never handled a murder before?"

"Not as a detective. I was at a few crime scenes when I was in the Air Police, but mostly just doing crowd control."

"Don't worry about it. This is only the third murder case I've handled in the six years on Mars. Fights and knifings, sure, but not real 'whodunit' sort of murders. So if you see anything that I miss, don't be afraid to speak up."

Ortiz smiled at him, "Don't worry, I won't."

The track got rougher after that and the conversation lapsed. McKernan took a stint driving after the first four hours, then they traded back a few hours after that. He was still tired after the long trip and didn't mind letting Ortiz do most of the driving. It gave him more time to think about how he was going to handle the investigation.

CHAPTER 4
DAY 2, 18:00-18:30

It was nearly dusk when they reached Station Alpha. Shadows cast by the setting sun brought the terrain into high relief. Alpha had been built on the rim of an escarpment overlooking a plain over a hundred meters below. One of the reasons the site had been chosen was for the varied stratigraphy the area provided allowing the geologists to explore millions of years into the Martian past. Someone with perhaps more art than science in mind had sited the main building so as to provide a magnificent view of a vista that extended for kilometers of some of the most interesting terrain on the planet. Unfortunately, at the moment, the lengthening shadows and the remains of the dust storm obscured most of it.

The main part of the station consisted of four large buildings arranged in the form of a "T" with the top of the "T" running parallel to the rim of the escarpment. The junction of the "T" was the administration building which contained not only the data processing center, conference room and storage, but also the dining and recreational facilities of the base. Each of the arms of the "T" was a residence wing, one for men and one for women. The leg was given over to labs and workshops as well as the offices of the chief scientist and the executive assistant. The three branch buildings were connected to the central one through short tunnels provided with airlocks. A number of outbuildings were scattered around the site as well, arranged as their purpose and functions dictated.

Ortiz pulled up to a line of vehicles that were parked alongside the lab wing. An airlock at the end of that building provided access to the station and suiting up, they exited the buggy and entered the lock.

Dr. William MacKensie, the chief scientist and administrator for the base was waiting for them when the airlock cycled. He was an older man, in his early sixties, tall and lean. MacKensie was known as "the grand old man of Martian science" with good reason, he'd been the geologist on the first scientific mission to Mars twenty five years earlier and for all intents and purposes had never left the planet since, except for short visits to Earth.

He extended his hand to McKernan and said, "I'm William MacKensie. I believe we've met before on one or two occasions, Inspector. I'm sorry your visit couldn't be on happier terms."

"Policemen rarely are called on when there isn't trouble, Doctor," McKernan responded. MacKensie had a reputation for calm and graciousness under the most difficult circumstances. "This is constable Elena Ortiz who will be assisting me in the investigation."

"Welcome, constable. We, too, have met before." Ortiz nodded.

"What do you want to do first, Inspector? Get started right away? Get settled first? I expect you'll be with us for several days at least?"

"Has the crime scene been secured?"

"Yes. I locked the room as soon as I was sure James was dead. Not that there was much doubt of that. I also had Philips lower the heating in the office to preserve the body. I hope that was all right?"

"After this long, it wouldn't have made much different," McKernan responded. "And I think we'd all be happy to minimize decomposition." Living in closed environments, Martians could be finicky about unpleasant smells.

"Just so," MacKensie said.

"If we could be shown our quarters and given a few minutes to freshen up, it would be appreciated. And then if I could meet with everyone in say half an hour?"

"That sounds reasonable. I'll show you to your rooms and then get everyone assembled. Fortunately, we've got plenty of space this time of the year. I've put Constable Ortiz in the women's wing if that is ok."

"Fine," McKernan answered. He hadn't thought about it before, but having Ortiz bunk with the other women might be a plus. They might say things to her that they wouldn't to a man.

MacKensie led them down the central corridor of the lab building to the airlock joining it to the admin building. McKernan noticed that the last door before the airlock had a freshly installed padlock on it. The corresponding door on the other side of the corridor was open to reveal a small cluttered but orderly office.

"I take it that most doors don't have locks?"

"Only the medical stores. As you can see, not even my office has a lock on it and I usually leave the door open unless I'm concentrating. Or trying to nap." MacKensie's humor was dry but genuine.

"The airlock hatches between buildings are always kept closed," the scientist said as he worked the handle to open the lock. As he opened the hatch an alarm began to ping and a light above the lock flashed. It wasn't overly loud, but it was hard to ignore. McKernan expected that the sound carried throughout the building. It stopped when they had stepped through into the lock and closed the hatch behind them.

"It's the only way we can get some of these people to remember to close the hatches," MacKensie said with a chuckle.

"Is there any record kept of the airlocks cycling?" McKernan asked.

"Yes, there is. Almost everything having to do with life support is monitored and recorded on a computer in the data center. The time is noted and a picture is taken of whoever uses the lock," he answered. "I've checked. This lock never opened between the time James entered the lab building around midnight until I entered just before I found the body."

"Is the visual record full motion or a still?" McKernan asked.

"It's a still image," MacKensie responded. Pointing he said, "You can see the camera there just over the hatch."

There was a small camera mounted on a bracket above the hatch on the inside of the lock pointing down at where a person would normally stand as they entered from that side. There was a matching camera pointing towards the hatch on the other side of the lock.

"And there was no one else in the lab building at that time?"

"No one. I'd wandered through the labs minutes before on my way to bed."

The other side of the lock opened onto a short corridor at the end of which was a large room with chairs and tables. A set of windows along wall gave a view over the edge of the escarpment.

"This is the dining hall/recreation room," MacKensie described. "The kitchen is to the right of this corridor and the sick bay and medical stores to the left." There was an open door looking into each. Once they were into the dining room, they could see corridors leading off in either direction.

"The conference room is to the right and the library is to the left on the side of the corridors towards the cliff," MacKensie said pointing in either direction. "The data center is across from the library, food stores are across from the conference room. The dormitory wings are through the airlocks at the end of each corridor. The Men's is that way, the womens' is the other," MacKensie said as he pointed. McKernan noted that from most of the dining room a person would have a clear view of each of the airlocks.

"I'll have everyone assemble in here, in a half an hour or so. Constable if you go through that lock Molly will show you your room. Inspector, if you'll follow me—"

When McKernan returned to the dining room the residents of Station Alpha were gathered sitting around the various tables. He noted that the four youngest scientists were all sitting together at a centrally located table. The others were paired off or sitting singly.

"Ladies and gentlemen, for those of you who don't know me, I am Chief Inspector McKernan of the Trust Authority Police and I am here to investigate the death of James Augustyn. This is Constable Ortiz who will be assisting me."

He noticed one of the four sitting together make a comment to his fellows. "Do you have something to say, Dr. Chen?"

If he was abashed, the scientist didn't show it. "Sorry, I guess it's just that when they said an inspector was coming I was expecting someone with a monocle and a deerstalker hat."

"This is not a detective novel. A man has been killed. And I will remind each of you that the murderer is one of the twelve people in this room. You are all suspects, and that includes you, Dr. Chen."

That seemed to get Chen's attention. McKernan noticed out of the corner of his eye that Ortiz was trying to hold back a grin.

"I called you all together to explain my procedures and exactly what is going to happen over the next day or two.

That is unless one of you wants to save us all a lot of trouble and admit to the murder."

There was a moment of silence as each of the suspects looked around to see if any of the others was going to speak up.

"No takers? Well I didn't expect it would be that easy. Alright. I've spent the last day and a half traveling and I'm tired, so I won't need any of you tonight. Tomorrow, Constable Ortiz and I will begin taking formal statements from each of you and asking a bunch of questions. It will be in your best interests to answer them as honestly as possible. As soon as this meeting breaks up, the constable and I will be examining the scene of the crime. I want all of you to stay out of the lab wing until we have completed our examination. I hope to be finished with that tonight, so it should not greatly inconvenience anyone. Are there any questions?"

A tall, middle aged woman raised her hand.

"Prof. Oddsdottir?"

"Will we be able to leave the station tomorrow? The whole purpose of our being here is to make field studies and the weather has already put us almost two weeks behind."

"Surface expeditions will be fine once we have taken your statement. If you need to get a particularly early start tomorrow, you can schedule an early interview with Constable Ortiz. We will try to be as accommodating as possible. Any other questions?"

"No? Good. This is the point where normally I would say no one is to leave town, but given our circumstances, I don't think that will be necessary. Good Night."

Professor Oddsdottir and several of the others approached Ortiz to schedule the interviews.

"We delayed dinner until you arrived," MacKensie said. "Do you want to eat before you look at the body?"

"No. Why don't you let everyone have their dinner. Ortiz and I will grab something later. Sometimes it's better to see a corpse on an empty stomach. How are your forensic skills, constable?"

"I've had basic courses in the service and training for Mars. I know what all the equipment in the kit is for and how to use it, but I've never actually dealt with a crime scene before."

"Neither have I, constable. Doctor MacKensie, I think we're as ready as we're going to be."

"If you'll follow me, then," MacKensie said.

CHAPTER 6
DAY 2, 19:00-21:00

The station head lead them back through the lock to the lab building, stopping at the locked door McKernan had spotted when they first arrived.

"The room has remained undisturbed since you discovered the body?" McKernan asked.

"Yes. I shut the door as soon as I was sure that Augustyn was dead. I had Philips, our maintenance man, affix the hasp and lock. I've kept custody of the keys myself." He reached into a pocket and produced a pair of keys wired together which he handed to McKernan.

"Ortiz, you have the camera and crime scene kit?"

"Yes, right here," she said holding up a plastic case the size of a small suitcase.

"Alright, I'm going to open the door. Before we enter, I want you to take pictures of all of the room you can see from the doorway."

"Just give me a minute to get the camera ready," the constable replied. A moment later, after retrieving a digital camera with a zoom lens from the case she said, "I'm ready."

McKernan inserted the key into the padlock and turned it. The lock opened and he removed it from the hasp. Turning the door handle, he pushed the door open. The air in the room was considerably colder than the already cool air of the corridor. Inside, they could see a small, neat office. A small desk stood against the far wall, flanked by a bookcase and a file cabinet. Except for a computer terminal, the desk top was clear. In front of the desk was a chair, the only chair in the office. The body of a man was sitting in the chair slumped back against the seat. Embedded in the head of the man was the pointed end of a geologist's hammer, a small instrument about forty centimeters long.

After turning on the office lights the inspector stepped back to let Ortiz take pictures. She went about the task efficiently and thoroughly, taking pictures of the desk, the floor, the walls and the ceiling, and then adjusting the zoom lens for a close up of the head.

"I'm done, sir, unless there is anything else you want me to take a picture of."

"Not at the moment. Doctor, if you will remain here for the moment."

McKernan entered the room, being careful to not touching anything. He circled to the side of the desk to look at the front of the body. The eyes were wide open, as was the mouth as if in surprise. Except for the hammer sticking out of the skull, there was no sign of violence. There was very little blood.

"Ortiz, could you hand me a pair of gloves and an evidence bag?"

"Here they are."

"Before I remove the hammer I want you to take pictures of the body from the front and both sides. Also a close up of the wound and the handle of the hammer."

While he waited for the constable to take the pictures McKernan put on the gloves. When Ortiz stepped back, he grasped the hammer gently with his right hand, holding the bag in his left. Carefully he worked the weapon out of the wound. The point was embedded almost up to the haft. Whoever had wielded it had used a great deal of force. Freeing the tip he dropped the hammer into the bag and sealed it.

Though meant as a tool, it made a deadly looking weapon. It had a metal haft about forty centimeters long with a two ended head. One end of the head extended about five centimeters and ended in a flat surface, the other was a gently curved spike about twelve centimeters long. The spike was what had been embedded in the skull. Bits of brain still stuck to the point.

"Tag it and store it. We can check for fingerprints later. Take pictures of anything you haven't already."

Ortiz took the bag gingerly; it wasn't clear whether it was from repugnance or a desire to protect the integrity of the evidence. She wrote a label and affixed it to the bag before stowing it in the forensics case.

McKernan turned his attention to the computer terminal on the desk. The screen was blank, but an LED on the case was lit. Using a pencil from his pocket he pressed one of the keys on the keyboard. The screen came to life. He read the document on the display, but it seemed to be just a report from one of the scientists at the station. There was nothing obviously incriminating about it.

"You can come in, now, doctor. Can you tell me if you see anything out of place, anything out of the ordinary."

MacKensie entered hesitantly, his eyes on the body. He looked around, but shook his head. "No, everything looks the same as the last time I was in here. Before I found the body that is. James was always very neat about his office, a trait I'm afraid I don't share. He was always chiding me about that."

"Oh, well. We'll have to do an inventory of the office. I don't suppose there would have been anything worth stealing in here, would there? Valuable samples, proprietary information, anything like that?"

"No, not in here. Any samples would have been locked in the sample room or one of the labs, not that we really have anything valuable in that line. Same with the information. This is a research station. Most of the results are already posted on the net and are available to the public. No one was doing any commercial investigations. At least not that I was aware of, and I've known most of people here for years."

"So we can rule out burglary as a motive," McKernan remarked sarcastically.

"Yes, I should think so. Inspector, I don' suppose there is any chance that James killed himself, is there?"

"Suicide? No I think we can rule that out as well. I just don't think it's possible to hit oneself in the back of the head with a hammer hard enough to drive it in that deep. The human arm just isn't meant to bend that way. It's pretty clear that whoever did it came up behind the victim and took a hefty down swing with the hammer like this—" McKernan demonstrated causing Mackensie to flinch.

"I didn't think so, it's just that I hate to think that one of the staff was capable of doing this."

"One of them must have. Unless you believe in Martians."

"Martians? Oh you mean the little green men that live outside," MacKensie responded. "No, I don't believe in them."

"Neither do I."

"Anything else you want me to do, Inspector?" Ortiz interrupted.

"Yeah. Put a bag over the victim's head to protect any evidence. Then do an ultra-violet scan for blood and dust the desk, and anything else that looks likely, for prints. The doctor and I will get out of your way. Let's step back into the corridor, doctor."

"What are you going to do with the body, Inspector?" MacKensie asked.

"We'll have to take it with us. I'll have to talk somebody in Mars City into doing an autopsy. We're really not set up for this kind of thing. Usually when somebody dies on Mars the cause is pretty obvious. There is no official Trust Authority Coroner or Medical Examiner. There's a pathologist at the hospital that can run a tox screen and write up a death report."

"A tox screen? You don't think drugs played a part?"

"I doubt it. And certainly not on the part of the victim. But if somebody took something recreational that caused him to run amok, it would make my job easier."

"Everybody at Station Alpha has had a rigorous background check before coming here. I can't believe one of them was a drug addict of any kind."

"Everyone on Mars has had a background check. I'm not accusing anyone, doctor. In fact I doubt that drugs were involved. As you say, it's too hard to get anything here from Earth and I'm not aware of anyone cooking up anything in that line in their spare time. It's just routine. And frankly, that's all I've got to go on at this time. I'll just follow the manual and keep poking my nose in things until something surfaces."

"And how long will that be?"

"You're guess is as good as mine, doctor."

"I found a few blood spatters. I took samples," Ortiz reported. "I found lots of prints. As close as I can figure they're from several dozen individuals. There's no sign that anything was wiped down."

"That's not surprising," MacKensie said. "This office has always been assigned to whoever handled most of the administrative details for the station. Everyone here currently and dozens of people who've been here in the past would have had occasion to go into this office."

"I didn't really expect the prints to show anything. It's just part of the procedure. If you're done here, Ortiz, let's get some dinner."

"I'm done with the forensic scans. Are we going to leave the body where it is?"

"I'd rather not. Dr. MacKensie, is there is someplace secure that we can store the body until we leave? I'd like to have this room available for further examination without having to work around a corpse."

"We do have a cold storage room for food stuffs," MacKensie said unenthusiastically.

"That should work," McKernan responded.

"The staff are going to love that," MacKensie said.

"Well, they just shouldn't have killed him then," McKernan answered. "We brought a body bag with us, in case anyone is squeamish. But we can deal with that in the morning. I'll put the lock back on. I'd just as soon not disturb things any more than necessary."

They sat at a small table in the dining portion of the commons room in the administration building eating dinner. After viewing the corpse, MacKensie looked a little queasy. Neither McKernan or Ortiz seemed to be bothered. The food was good by Mars standards, a beef stew with bread. Bread was a luxury on Mars. Growing grains of any sort took up a lot of space and water. There was butter, too.

McKernan reflected that the scientists at Station Alpha ate pretty well. Considering that most of what they were eating had been brought from Earth, this meal was costing someone a fortune. Even freeze dried, the shipping costs could have fed a person for a month if spent on local food. Of course there was no Martian beef and not much wheat. Even Ortiz, who seemed to be feeding pretty well at Junction 3 appreciated the dinner.

"What's your next step, Inspector?" MacKensie asked. "Is there anything I can do to help?"

"First thing is I'm going to get some sleep. I could use it. Then in the morning we'll start taking formal statements from everyone. Where they were from midnight until the time you discovered the body. If they know anything relevant. That sort of thing."

"Of course," the station head responded.

"Let me ask you one thing right now. Who do you think did it?"

"I find it hard to believe that any of the staff could have committed murder. I've known some of these people professionally for decades. Even the younger members of the staff were handpicked. Appointments to Station Alpha are highly coveted. The Trust Authority can afford to be highly selective. Everyone has been thoroughly screened for suitability as well as for academic credentials."

"And the non-scientific staff? What about them?"

"You know Trust Authority policy as well as anyone. Everyone who comes to Mars is vetted. Molly has been on Mars for years. She came up with her husband who was a pilot. She's been working at the station since its beginning. Besides, what could be her motive."

"What about Philips, the maintenance man."

"He's been at the station a couple of years. Very good man. He can fix just about anything, computers, vehicles, surface suits, you name it. Very reliable. I can't vouch for his initial screening, though. He came up initially to work for one of the mining concerns. Anglo-Martian, I think. He decided to stay when his contract with them was over. I was glad to hire him on. He had the highest recommendations. But it would have been the company that he first worked for that would have done the screening. Of course that would have been to Trust Authority standards. It should all be on his official records."

"So you can't think of anyone with a motive? Everybody liked Augustyn?"

MacKensie hesitated for a moment. "I can't really say that. James handled the administrative side of things. He tended to be a bit of a stickler for details. You know, the proper forms filled out correctly, budgets, that sort of thing. I'm sure there was some friction because of that. But not enough to kill him for, I'm sure."

"Go on. Was there any incident in particular?"

MacKensie looked troubled.

"If there's something, it's going to come out sooner or later," McKernan said. "It won't help matters if you are concealing something."

"I understand, Inspector. The problem is, it's nothing specific. The fact is Augustyn was something of a prick. He thought he was better than everyone because of his connections on Earth. He tended to lord it over the junior staff like Chen and Berlanescu. He was also a bit of a womanizer, as well. In the past, there have been complaints from some of the female scientists he's worked with, but James was always very careful not to say or do anything that would force action to be taken."

"Was that with any of the women currently at the station?"

"Not that I know of. Certainly not Molly or Sigrid. Sigrid would have eaten him for lunch if he had made improper advances. She's got a high enough standing on Earth that James couldn't have touched her. I don't think Molly was his type. He liked them younger."

"What about Toranaga? She's younger and looks quite attractive."

"She never made a complaint."

"Did his actions ever cause any jealousy from the male members of the staff?"

"Not officially, no. And I'm afraid that the younger members of the staff tend not to confide personal information to me. But, to be realistic, the station is a small world and it's hard to avoid tensions in that sort of environment."

"Is there anything else you might want to mention?"

MacKensie looked around nervously.

"Well, to be perfectly frank, James never was that great of a scientist. He was always much better at the political end of it. I've heard rumors that some of the research for his early papers, the ones that made his name, as it were, well that research might not all have been his. There certainly isn't anything spectacular about his more recent papers. And of course, a lot of the actual science would have been done by grad students and post docs working for him with James' name appearing as the lead investigator. But that's expected of a man in his position."

"I see. Well, thank you, Dr. MacKensie. That gives us some ideas to follow up on."

"If that is all, Inspector, I think I will retire now. It is getting late."

"Of course," McKernan answered. "Good night."

After he had left Ortiz said, "Well, that was interesting."

"Yes. The younger staff didn't like Augustyn because he threw his weight around. The women didn't like him because he was a pig, and none of the scientists thought much of him as a scientist and he might have stolen credit or research from any one of them. Basically, anyone at the station except for MacKensie might have a motive."

"Did you notice," Ortiz asked, "that while MacKensie seemed full of gossip, he never mentioned anyone in particular or got into specifics."

McKernan looked at the constable and smiled. "Yes, I did notice. As you said, interesting. It just might be that he's trying to protect his people. He seems like the type that would do that. But, personally, I think Dr. MacKensie knows more than he's letting on. He was right about one thing, though. It's time to get some sleep. We have a busy day ahead of us tomorrow."

CHAPTER 8
DAY 3, 07:00-08:00

When McKernan entered the dining hall the next morning he saw that MacKensie was already there. The station head was gazing out the large window at the sunrise.

"Good morning, Inspector. I see you're getting right to it. Incredible sight, isn't it," he said gesturing at the scene outside the window.

McKernan had to admit that it was a dramatic view. From the station's vantage point at the top of an escarpment overlooking a wide plain one could see for kilometers. The sun was rising over the rim of a crater in the distance, casting long shadows that threw every irregularity on the plain below into high relief.

"I never get tired of watching this," MacKensie said. "This is the reason that I insisted that the station be sited here. One can really get a sense of the splendors of the planet. I like to think that it inspires the scientists that come here."

"It is a magnificent sight," McKernan replied. He didn't know how much it served as an inspiration to the scientists, but there could be no doubting the view's effects on MacKensie. "You had a role in Station Alpha's origins?"

"You might say the station is my baby, Inspector. As you probably know, I was on all three of the original Martian Science Missions. One thing that I always regretted about those was the lack of continuity from one mission to the next. Once man started settling permanently on Mars I saw the opportunity for a permanent science post, a place where younger scientists could be mentored by those with more experience and where different specialties could interact with each other. Fortunately, I was in a position to influence things. You know, Inspector, Mars won't always be a frontier outpost. It will need to develop its own institutions. I envision Station Alpha as one day becoming the core of a University of Mars."

"But I don't want to bore you with my personal hobby horse," MacKensie interrupted himself. "You'll be interrogating everyone this morning?"

"I prefer to use the term interviewing. So far we don't have any reason to suspect a specific person. I just want to establish where everyone was that night, and what corroboration for each person's status there is. Standard routine police work."

"Forgive me, Inspector. I'm afraid all I know about police methods comes from novels and videos."

"That's the case with most people. Real police work is rarely as glamorous as it is in fiction. Mostly routine, filling in the blanks, eliminating possible suspects. That's what I hope to do today."

As they were talking, Ortiz had entered the room from the women's quarters.

"Morning, Dr. MacKensie. Sir."

"Good morning, Constable."

"If you'll excuse us, doctor, the constable and I need to get some breakfast before our first interview."

"Of course. Good luck on your work."

The breakfast menu was as good as that for dinner, eggs, a couple of sausage links, actual toast and butter. McKernan wondered what this case was doing to his cholesterol. He hadn't eaten so many eggs and so much pork since he'd left Earth. There was even orange juice. Ortiz seemed to be enjoying the meal as well.

"What's the plan for today, sir?" Ortiz asked when they'd finished eating.

"We'll interview each of the personnel in turn. I'll ask the questions. I want you to operate the recorder, but otherwise remain in the background."

"Sir?" Ortiz sounded disappointed.

"What I want them to do is focus on me and ignore you. That way you can observe them without their noticing. Also, if they think you're just here in a supporting role, somebody might open up to you later or let something slip when I'm not around. That's particularly important with the women."

"I understand, sir. I'm to be the little cop that wasn't there."

"Exactly. I want you to keep your eyes and ears open at all times. Somebody at this station killed Augustyn, and we need to find who. Now do you have the schedule? I believe Dr. Oddsdottir is up first."

They set up the equipment for the interviews in the conference room which they had requisitioned for the investigation. McKernan chose a table and placed a comfortable chair on either side. The camera for recording the interviews was placed behind him to his right. Ortiz sat in another chair at the end of the table to McKernan's left along with the recording equipment.

"If you're ready, let's begin," McKernan said.

Ortiz went to get the first interviewee, Dr. Sigrid Oddsdottir.

Interview –
Sigrid Oddsdottir
Day 3, 08:00-08:30

Dr. Oddsdottir looked every inch the descendent of her Viking ancestors who had settled Iceland some twelve centuries earlier. In her late forties, her body still retained that lean but muscular athleticism that seems to be unique to the Scandinavians. Her blonde hair was starting to gray and was worn long and straight. It was evident that when she was younger she would have been a great beauty; now her features had hardened into a kind of classical elegance.

"Thank you for seeing me so early, Inspector," she said, instinctively taking charge. She spoke in very correct English that still had a slight Scandinavian accent overlaid on top of that of the Canadian plains. McKernan smiled to himself. Dr. Oddsdottir was not someone to be pushed around. "I'll answer any of your questions, but I would appreciate it if we can keep this brief. The weather has put me way behind schedule, and I only have a limited time before I must return to Earth."

"I understand, doctor," McKernan said politely. "I'll try to get straight to the point. To start with, could you give me an account of your movements on the night Dr. Augustyn was killed."

"I ate dinner at the usual hour, about 19:00. Nils, Dr. Jensen that is, and I watched a video in the lounge for an hour or so after dinner and then I retired to my quarters. Except for trips to the bathroom I remained there until I went to breakfast around 07:30. I think I entered the dining room about the time Dr. MacKensie came from the lab and reported that Dr. Augustyn was dead."

"Do you have any witnesses? I'm not accusing you of lying, of course, but the more corroboration I have as to times and such the better."

"I think I ran into Sarah Toranaga in the hall around 22:00. And of course there is Nils."

"I'm mostly concerned with the period between 24:00 and 07:30 the next morning."

"Yes, I understand. Nils spent the night in my room."

McKernan raised an eyebrow while Ortiz sat impassively at the recorder.

"You needn't look so shocked, inspector. Nils and I are old friends and colleagues. Neither of us has any permanent attachments. Mars is a long way from anywhere and even geologists get lonely. As long as we are discrete about it, no one seems to mind. Sarah and Boris occasionally did the same thing, and Molly certainly had no objections."

"Well, if the two of you can vouch for each other, that makes my job easier," McKernan said in response. "Do you know if Dr. Federenkov was with Dr. Toranaga that night?"

"No, I don't believe he was, but then they were also very discrete."

"Did you know Dr. Augustyn before this trip to Mars?"

"Inspector, the world of geologists specializing in Mars is not a big one. Everyone knows everyone else, even if only from conferences, but in fact I did know Dr. Augustyn from before."

The way she said it made McKernan think there might be more to the story.

"Could you elaborate?"

"It was when I was a post-doc. Dr. Augustyn was a visiting professor for a term. We came into contact then. He made, how shall I say it, 'advances' towards me. I turned him down. The results were not pleasant."

"Go on."

"You must understand, that a post-doc has no permanent position, no tenure. I was working for someone else on their grant. Dr. Augustyn was at first very charming. He was an up and coming man in the field, though later I learned that maybe not for his own research. He said that he could be a big help to my career. That may or may not have been true, but I felt I could do well enough on my own merits. Besides, the more I came to know Dr. Augustyn, the less charming he seemed. He really was a pig and not nearly as brilliant as his reputation would lead you to believe. I turned him down. In no uncertain terms. He took it badly. I don't think he liked being opposed. He said that he would ruin my career. I don't know if there was much he could have done, but as I said, it's a small community and rumors do get around. Even in this day there still is a certain amount of sexism in academe and it doesn't do you any good for a woman to be known as a slut or a tease."

"What did you do?" McKernan asked.

"I went to my boss, the man who's grant I was working under, and reported the incident."

"And what did he do?"

"He told me not to worry. There wasn't much he could do because Augustyn was visiting from another institution and a formal disciplinary action wasn't practical. Augustyn would be going back to Australia at the end of the term. My boss said it was an unfortunate situation, but that he would make sure that my career wasn't impacted."

"And was it?"

"No, I would have to say it wasn't. If Augustyn said anything, it didn't go far. I think my boss may have said something to him in private. Even then, he was a big man in the field. Anyway, he recommended me for an opening at the University of Edmonton, and I got the appointment at the start of the next academic year. Tenure followed in due course. I think my boss has followed my career ever since. I know he recommended me for my first field season on Mars."

"Just for the record, who was your boss at that time?" McKernan asked.

"Oh, did I forget to mention that. It was Dr. MacKensie. He really can be an old dear at times." Her face actually cracked a smile at the thought.

"Is there anything else that you can add that might shed light on Dr. Augustyn's murder?"

"No. Not that I can think of. I can't think of anyone who really liked him, but I can't think of anyone who would have killed him. Certainly not one of the people here at Station Alpha."

"Well, then, thank you, doctor. I think that will be all for the time being. You've been very helpful."

After Dr. Oddsdottir rose and left the room, Ortiz looked at McKernan, wondering just what conclusions he had drawn from the interview.

INTERVIEW –
NILS JENSEN
DAY 3, 08:30-09:00

If Sigrid Oddsdottir looked like a middle aged Viking shield maiden, Nils Jensen looked like a Danish toymaker. He had a thin, wiry build, a seamed face dominated by a prominent nose and light blue eyes. His hair was a thinning grey worn moderately long. In an age where surgical correction was common he still wore a pair of wire-rimmed glasses. His face carried an air of mild amusement when he entered the conference room where the interviews were being conducted.

"I've never actually been questioned by the police before, Inspector. That is the correct title, isn't it? Like something out of an English mystery," he said in barely accented English.

"It's Chief Inspector, actually," McKernan answered. "I think the titles were chosen intentionally. The Trust Authority wanted to avoid anything along military lines, and terms like sheriff or marshal were deemed too American for the committee's taste. I suspect the committee responsible chose 'inspector' because it makes me sound like a mid-level civil servant. Or, as you say, they may have had a fondness for British detective novels."

"I suspect you're right. In my experience, committees rarely make decisions for logical reasons," Jensen responded with a smile.

Seemingly without trying, Jensen had prevented the inspector from taking charge of the interview, McKernan thought to himself. He also thought that he noted a faint smile on Ortiz's face as she operated the recorder.

"Well, I know that you want to get back to work, so I'll try to make this as brief as possible.   To start, why don't you tell me what you did on the night Dr. Augustyn was murdered?"

"Let's see," Jensen said. "I had dinner at the usual time, 19:00 or so. I think I watched a video in the lounge for an hour or so after that, and then I went to bed. I got up in the morning at 07:00 or 07:30 and went to breakfast. That's when Dr. MacKensie came into the dining room and announced that James was dead."

"So you went to bed around 21:00?"

"Probably more like 22:00 or a little later. As I said I watched a video with Sigrid, we talked a bit with a few of the others both before and after, and then we went to bed."

"Together?" McKernan asked.

Dr. Jensen raised an eyebrow. "Yes, if you must know, we went to Sigrid's room and I spent the night in her bed."

"Are you in the habit of doing that?"

"Not infrequently. Sigrid and I are old friends. Neither one of us is married or has a current significant other. Mars is a lonely place. We are discrete, and no one else seems to mind. As there are only three women at the station, it makes sense to use her room rather than my own. There are fewer people to disturb and more space between occupied rooms.   Sarah and Boris have the same arrangement, though probably on a less frequent basis, so she has no objections, and I don't think Molly minds either. The conditions at a research station in space do not encourage the prudish."

"So you retired to Dr. Oddsdottir's room around 22:00 or a little later and stayed there until morning. Did you hear or see anyone else during that time?"

"I think Sarah was already in her room when we went to bed, but I could hear her moving around. I think she stayed up quite late reading. Molly came in after we did and went to bed fairly quickly. She snores a bit. She gets up quite early to prepare breakfast. About 05:30 or so on that occasion if I remember correctly."

"But other than that, you didn't hear or see anyone entering or leaving the women's wing?"

"No. But then I tend to be a sound sleeper."

"Is there anything else that you can tell me that might shed light on who killed Dr. Augustyn?" McKernan asked.

"No," Dr. Jensen hesitated. "Well, I don't like to speak ill of the dead, but James wasn't particularly well liked. I know Sigrid thought he was a pig."

"And you, Dr. Jensen?"

"No. I didn't like him either."

"Was there a particular reason?" Mckernan asked.

"Yes, there was. Dr. Augustyn caused the breakup of my marriage, though I suspect that in the end I was equally at fault."

"Would you care to explain?"

"I might as well. It was sure to come out sooner or later. Sigrid and Mac know the details and Breaker was witness to the whole sordid proceedings. It was about fifteen years ago. I'd been married ten years at the time, though it wasn't going that well. Being the wife of a field geologist isn't as romantic as it sounds, particularly when that geologist spends extended time away on expeditions to Greenland or Mars.

"Anyway, I had arranged a term as a visiting lecturer at the University of Sydney. Breaker had a hand in that. He knew some people. I thought a few months in an exotic locale would help my marriage, and compared to Copenhagen, Sydney is certainly exotic. Of course, the reality was that I spent a lot of time in meetings and colloquium and taking trips to the outback to see interesting bits of geology, so my wife was left to herself a lot. Now I want you to keep in mind that she was quite attractive then. Still is. Of course, James, who was vice chairman of the department at the time, thought it was his duty to entertain her. Show her the sites and that sort of thing. Well it ended up being a lot more than that. The two of them, James and my wife, ended up having a rather torrid affair. Not very discretely, either. Universities are never that big of a place, even in a big city like Sydney. People saw them together. There was talk. It became a topic of gossip.

"I found out, of course. People who were my friends saw them together and told me. Even then, James wasn't particularly well liked. There was the inevitable row. In the end, my wife left Sydney early. Went back to Denmark and filed for a divorce. I didn't contest it. Didn't really want to, to put it bluntly."

"So you had reason not to like Dr. Augustyn?" McKernan asked pointedly.

"Yes, but not so much as to want to kill him," Dr. Jensen said resignedly. "The fact is my marriage was doomed at that point and a separation or divorce was inevitable. The affair was just an excuse to get it over with. My overwhelming emotion about the whole business is one of sadness, not anger. Still, my relations with James have never been cordial since. He could at least have had the decency to be discrete."

"And did Dr. Oddsdottir have any part in this 'business' as you put it," McKernan asked sternly.

"No. Certainly not. We'd known each other professionally, of course, before that. Our interests overlap. But it wasn't until a few years later when we were on an expedition together that we became an 'item' as they say. It's not really anything full time, or exclusive, you understand, our schedules don't permit that, just when it's convenient. Still, Sigrid is quite a woman, even if she is a bit intimidating at times."

"So you were ok with Dr. Augustyn?" McKernan asked. "He never tried to get between you and Dr. Oddsdottir?"

"Sigrid would never permit that. She loathed him. That's actually the reason we hooked up. We were sitting around having a couple of drinks after work and the subject of James came up. I think it was actually some comment Breaker made about never turning your back on him. We ended up comparing notes and then hit the sack together. Greenland's a damned cold place at night."

"So you, Dr. Oddsdottir, and Dr. Morand were on an expedition to Greenland, together?"

"Oh, yes. Cold climate geology is really a very small world. Everybody knows everybody else. As a matter of fact, I think Dr. MacKensie was there for a bit as well. It was the last time he was back on Earth. Except for that last short trip."

"Was there something exceptional about that?"

"Didn't you know? Only that he had to return to Mars in a hurry. He'd spent so much time in the lower gravity of Mars that his heart couldn't take the strain of Earth weight anymore. Not that he minded. He loves this place. It just gave him an excuse to move here permanently."

"Well, thank you, Dr. Jensen. You've been quite frank and helpful. Is there anything else you can tell me that might be pertinent?"

"No. I don't think so."

"That will be all then," McKernan said. Dr. Jensen stood up and offered his hand to shake.

"That was actually rather painless, Inspector. Good day."

Interview –
Roger "Breaker" Morand
Day 3, 09:00-09:30

Roger Morand was an athletic man of middle height in his early forties. He looked both tanned and windblown, which was a good trick on Mars where outdoor exposure would kill you in minutes. He was dressed in slightly rumpled clothing that was trying to say "scientist on an expedition." From his files, McKernan had gleaned the fact that in addition to his academic duties he acted as the host for a successful television science program. He was certainly trying to look the part.

"Good-day, Inspector," he said with a broad smile as he sat down. He nodded affably at Ortiz. She nodded back and appeared to be busy with the recorder. "What can I do for you?"

"Thank you for sparing me some time, Dr. Morand," McKernan responded formally. After Jensen, he didn't want Morand to take charge of the interview. "I appreciate it."

"Call me Breaker. Everyone does."

"Breaker?"

"It's an old Aussie thing. Goes back to some bloke in the Boer War."

"Ok, Breaker," McKernan said, trying to make it sound forced. "Let's start by you telling me what you were doing the night Dr. Augustyn was killed."

"Simple enough. After dinner I went to my room and did some reading. I think I nodded off about 23:00. I got up the next morning about 07:15. It looked like the weather was breaking and we might actually be able to get out and do some real work. I went down to the dining room about 07:30 or so. I got there just after Mac came in and announced that Augustyn was dead. That's really about all I know."

"Can anyone verify this. You understand that I don't doubt your story, but the more I can corroborate the facts the more it will help me eliminate people as suspects."

"Sure. Well, I wasn't sleeping with anyone, but Boris stopped by my room about 21:30. We talked for ten, fifteen minutes. Discussing what we might be able to do the next day if the weather would let us. He left and I heard him go down the hall to his room. It's a couple of doors down from mine. Like I said, I went to sleep about an hour after that. Slept through until morning."

"You didn't get up in the middle of the night to go to the bathroom or anything?"

"No. Though I think I heard someone get up around 04:00. I think it was Mac. Oh, and a little after 02:00 the four youngsters must have finally tired of playing cards because I heard them going to their rooms. Noisy bunch of blokes. I yelled at them to keep it down."

"But none of them saw you?"

"No. I just rolled over and went back to sleep."

"Thank you, that's been really helpful."

"Glad to oblige."

"How well did you know Dr. Augustyn?" McKernan asked.

"Well, I knew him," Morand answered. "He was on the faculty at the University of Queensland when I was there working on my doctorate. "Not that I hung out with him, or anything. I was just a lowly grad student and even then he was starting to make a name for himself. Since then, we bump into each other at conferences and things. Can't help that. There aren't that many people in the field."

"Dr. Augustyn's research is similar to yours?"

"Broadly speaking. What he does of it these days." Morand didn't sound so much bitter as dismissive.

"I take it you didn't particularly like Dr. Augustyn?"

"James was what you might call a right wanker. He'd screw over anyone to further his own career. He'd try to screw the sheilas, too, and he wasn't particular if they were attached or not. I can't think of many people that liked James."

"I see. Did you have any particular grievance against him?"

"Me? You're a sharp one. Well I guess it's going to come out from someone. It's not like it's a closely guarded secret."

"Go on," McKernan encouraged.

"It was just after I had gotten my Ph. D. I was trying to get an appointment to the Second Martian Science Expedition. I'd been working on this paper. It would have been my ticket to the trip." McKernan noted that Morand had dropped the Aussie affectations if not the accent.

"It was pretty good stuff, if I say so myself. I'd kept it pretty much to myself. Even my Ph. D. advisor didn't know the details. So you can imagine my surprise when just as I was going to send it to the evaluation committee for the expedition I open a journal and find a nearly identical paper authored by you guessed it, James Augustyn. Same data, same conclusions, even the same bloody language in some cases."

"And there was no chance that Dr. Augustyn had coincidentally come up with the same results."

"Not a chance in hell. There were just too many similarities. The only thing I could figure is that he had had someone hack into the University computer network and steal a draft of the paper and the data. Later I heard rumors that he had been blackmailing some bloke at the computer centre."

"Well there really wasn't anything I could do. Augustyn was already a name. He was on the selection committee for the expedition. I talked to my advisor, but he told me not to make waves. He said no one would believe me and it would ruin my career."

"So what did you do?"

"I went to MacKensie. He was the scientific head of the expedition. He was very sympathetic. I could tell that he believed me. But he told me that without proof it would be my word against Augustyn. Augustyn had too many friends in high places. He always was good at politics. Mac said to let it drop and he'd try to make it right."

"And did he?"

"Mac was as good as his word. Maybe better. He called in a favor with one of his friends and wrangled me a spot on an expedition to Antarctica to study Erebus. It wasn't Mars, but I got a couple of good papers out of it and a tenured position at Sydney. In the end, it was probably better for my career than having been a junior scientist doing grunt work on the Second expedition. By the time of the Third Expedition, I had enough of a reputation that Mac was able to get me a posting as a senior researcher."

"So you never tried to get back at Augustyn even though he nearly ruined your career?"

"What was the point? I had no proof. And after I cooled off in Antarctica I was too busy doing real work. I had tenure. I had a solid reputation in my field. For Christ's sake, I even had my own Vidie show. I'm a celebrity. More people have seen me standing on Erebus in a parka or on Olympus Mons in a surface suit than ever saw James."

"Still, I'm surprised that, given your feelings, you were here at Station Alpha at the same time as Augustyn."

"I wasn't any too happy about that when I found out, but I had made a promise to Mac. He wanted someone sound to mind the youngsters. He's getting on a bit and can't do everything, and he certainly didn't want to trust them to Augustyn. Besides, he made me a promise. He's going to arrange to get me the appointment as chief scientist on the Io expedition. James could never top that. Not with people that count."

"Look, I won't lie to you, Inspector. I didn't shed a tear when Mac announced that Augustyn was dead, but I didn't do it. I don't know who did, and I'm not sure I'd tell you if I did. Frankly I think they should get a medal for ridding the solar system of a prime bastard."

"Can I take it then that you have nothing more to add?" McKernan asked.

"I think that's a fair statement. Can I go now? I've got work to do."

"Yes, that will be all for the moment. Thank you for your cooperation."

"Good-day, mates," Morand said as he got up, the smile back on his face.

After he left, McKernan looked at Ortiz.

"Sir, I don't think he did it," the constable remarked. "He was too open about everything."

"I think you may be right."

INTERVIEW – SARAH TORANAGA
DAY 3, 10:00-10:30

Doctor Sarah Toranaga took her place in the chair opposite McKernan with the lithe grace of an athlete. Though obviously part Japanese, there were certainly other races in her ancestry. She was tall, thin, fit and looked a few years younger than her age of 32. McKernan noticed that unlike the pasty complexion most people on Mars acquired, Toranaga's skin still seemed to maintain the healthy glow of her native southern California.

"Thank you for coming, Dr. Toranaga," McKernan said perfunctorily. "We're just trying to establish where everybody was on the night of the murder."

"Well, I had dinner in the dining hall with everybody else. I went back to my room in the women's residence wing. It must have been about 20:00 or maybe a little later. I sat up reading for awhile. I think it was about 01:30 or 02:00 when I finally turned off the light."

"So late? It must have been a good book," McKernan commented.

Toranaga grinned sheepishly. "I was reading The Uncorrupted Corpse by Ezekiel Handler. I admit an addiction to sensational mysteries. Have you read any of his works?

"One or two. I don't have much time for reading. When I do, it's mostly older stuff like R. Austin Freeman or Freeman Wills Crofts. So you were in your room until morning."

"Yes, except for a trip to the bathroom."

"Do you remember the time when Dr. Oddsdottir and Mrs. MacDougal came in?"

"Sigrid went to her room a little after I did. I think Nils might have been with her. Hers is the one at the end of the corridor. Mine's in the middle on the other side. With only three women here now we've spaced things out for privacy. Molly came to bed about 22:00 or maybe a little later. She always cleans up the kitchen and preps for breakfast before coming to bed."

"And her room is where?"

"It's the first one on the right as you enter. It's the closest to the kitchen."

"And you didn't hear either of them get up in the night?"

"Not while I was awake. Sigrid would have had to walk right past my room. The door was shut, but they don't provide much sound proofing. As to Molly, well, she's a dear, but she snores. I could still hear her when I finally turned out the light. I fell asleep pretty quickly, and didn't wake up until the alarm went off at 07:20."

"That's very helpful, Dr. Toranaga. Do you mind telling me how you came to be at Station Alpha? You understand I'm just trying to build a picture of who everyone is."

"That's easy. Dr. MacKensie read a paper I wrote as a post doc. He liked what he read and knew the professor I was working for at the time. Though it has been years since he's been back to Earth, he still maintains contacts with a lot of people there. Anyway, he liked what he read and contacted me to see if I was interested in working on Mars for a year. I jumped at the chance. I don't know if you understand how important having worked a stint on Mars can be for your career. I've already had two offers of a position with tenure when I get back to Earth. Dr.

MacKensie helped get me a grant for the year and work out the other details."

"Is there any special reason for this attention on Dr. MacKensie's part?" McKernan asked.

Toranaga looked surprised for a moment and then laughed. "It's nothing like that. Dr. MacKensie is famous for finding young researchers and arranging for them to spend time on Mars. I know he did the same for David Chen and Dieter. Tony worked for an ex-grad student of Dr. MacKensie. From what I've heard he helped arrange Breaker's place on his first stint on Mars. That's just what he does. Either he finds a paper that he likes or one of his friends mentions someone they think might do well and then he arranges things. He's probably played a part in getting half the university researchers that have ever been on Mars their stint."

"I see," McKernan said. "So there was nothing unprofessional about it?"

Toranaga laughed again. "Dr. MacKensie? He's old enough to be my grandfather. Besides, I think the only thing that he really loves is Mars."

"I'm sorry, Dr. Toranaga. I didn't mean to imply anything about either one of you. I'm just trying to figure things out."

"It's OK. The only one who's been unprofessional was Dr. Augustyn. He tried to hit on me more than once. He claimed that he could do wonders for my career. He was always talking about the big position he was getting after this trip and how he would look after those he considered his friends."

"I take it you spurned his advances?"

"What a quaint way of expressing it, but yes, I shut him down fast and repeatedly. When I first got here Sigrid took me aside and warned me about Augustyn. I think she had some bad experiences with him in the past. For that matter Breaker told me never to turn my back on him."

"How are your relations with the other members of the staff."

"Oh, we all get along pretty well. Sigrid and Nilss and Breaker are of course senior, but they don't push it. And the young guys joke around a lot. David Chen likes practical jokes and Tony is always trying to play the cool Italian stud. Dieter and Sean play along, but it's just blowing off steam. But really, everybody is too much tied up in their work."

"I notice that you've left out Dr. Federenkov—" McKernan said.

Toranaga blushed. "I knew Boris back on Earth. He spent a year at my university on a visiting fellowship. We got to know each other. Well. If you must know, we've got a bit of a thing going. I don't know if it will amount to anything when we go back to Earth, but we're here for a year and there aren't a lot of other distractions. I like him. He's brilliant--and sweet."

"So no problems."

"No. We get along great. We're discrete and people are pretty cool about things and look the other way. We're all adults."

"What about the non-scientific staff? What can you tell me about them?"

"Molly's a dear. Like an aunt. She takes care of us. I don't really know that much about Jason Philips. He's pretty quiet. Spends most of his time with his machines and things. Ok, maybe he's a little creepy at times, but I've never had a problem with him."

"Is there anything else you can tell me that might have a bearing on the case?"

"Not that I can think of. You know, scientists can get passionate, but mostly about their work. I don't think anyone here really considered Dr. Augustyn to be a scientist anymore. He was just a bureaucrat we had to deal with. An annoyance, if you understand what I'm saying."

It was McKernan's turn to smile. "I think so. I think that will be all for the moment. I'd like to thank you again for your help."

"Any time, Inspector," she said as she left.

Interview –
Boris Federenkov
Day 3, 10:30-11:00

The first thing that McKernan noticed about Boris Federenkov was the intensity of his eyes. They gave an impression of extreme concentration and focus. The Russian Geologist was himself a slight figure of middle height. Unlike the other scientists at the station he was neither overtly athletic or wiry in his physique. The detective wondered whether that was due to his personal habits or a result of growing up in a Russia suffering from one of its periodic economic collapses. With his delicate, boyish features and unruly brown hair he was not unhandsome, but McKernan guessed that it was his intellect that attracted Dr. Toranaga. From his file, Federenkov had already made a name for himself professionally and was viewed by many to be one of the up and coming figures in the field of planetary geology. At 35, his age placed him between the younger card players and the older hands like Morand and the Scandinavians.

As he entered the room a wary expression crossed his face, the age old Russian distrust of the police.

"Sit down, Dr. Federenkov, "McKernan said, trying to reassure the other with a friendly tone. "I'll try to keep this as brief as possible."

"Yes, thank you." Unlike most of the other scientists, his English was heavily accented.

"To start with, could you please tell me what you did the night Dr. Augustyn died?"

"I had dinner with the others at usual time. 19:00. Then I went to my room. I had work to do on paper I am preparing. Not on results from this expedition, but theoretical work I've been doing. I worked until midnight or so, then slept. I woke at 07:00, took a shower, and went to breakfast at 07:30."

"And after you went to your room, did you see or talk to anyone?" McKernan asked.

"When I heard Breaker go to room I went to talk to him for few minutes about next day's work. You understand that the storm had kept us from working outside for over a week. As storm was dying down, we wanted to get outside. That was maybe 21:00, 21:30. I'm not sure exactly. In morning, I saw Breaker and David in the bathroom."

"And did you hear when any of the others came in to bed?"

"Dr. MacKensie walked by my room about 24:00. About the time I went to sleep. I heard David and Tony came in late but I didn't bother to look at the time. The others may have come in about same time."

"Thank you. That pretty much agrees with what everyone else has said. Did you know Dr. Augustyn before this trip to Mars?"

"No. I must have been introduced at conferences, but I don't remember. I wasn't particularly interested in his work. Very ordinary. Not related to mine, you understand. He was always more interested in how you say, the politics, funding, grants, that kind of thing, not the science. I know people said not to cross Dr. Augustyn. He could make trouble for career. But me, I'm more interested in science."

"And Dr. Toranaga? Did you know her before this trip?"

A smile crossed the Russian's face. "Yes. I spent year at same university as she works at two years ago. She showed

me around. Help me with my English. We became friends.
She is not just pretty face. Very good scientist."

"Did her coming to Mars influence your coming?"

"No. That was Dr. MacKensie's suggestion. He has liked
several of my papers. Asked if I would like to work on Mars.
It is not an opportunity one turns down.   Not when
MacKensie asks. When I found out Sarah will be here, it is
like, what, bonus."

"Will you be going back to Russia when you return to
Earth?"

"No. I have appointment at Caltech. Professorship.
That will be nice. I will be close to Sarah. Excuse me, are
these questions relevant?" Federenkov asked suspiciously.

"I'm just trying to understand how the people at Station
Alpha relate to each other. How did you get along with Dr.
Augustyn?"

"Not very well. Dr. Augustyn was not nice man. He said
some things to Dr. Toranaga that he shouldn't have. He
tried to make difficulties for me, too. He said he would send
me back to Russia. Get Caltech offer rescinded. I tried to
ignore him. I talked to Dr. MacKensie. He said it was just
Dr. Augustyn's way. That I was much better scientist than
him and that I didn't have to worry."

"Still, his actions towards Dr. Toranaga must have
concerned you."

"Dr. Toranaga is able woman. She can take care of
herself. We didn't talk much about Dr. Augustyn."

"So after dinner, you didn't spend any more time with
Dr. Toranaga?"

"No. We had dinner together, then we went to our
rooms. She knew I was working on paper. She understands
work."

"I'm just trying to clarify everyone's activities that
night."

"Why? You think maybe I snuck up behind Dr. Augustyn and buried hammer in his head? Is that what you think? Well I didn't. I was working. Then I slept." There was a finality of that statement that led McKernan to believe there was no use pursuing the matter further.

"Can you think of anyone who might have had a motive to kill Dr. Augustyn?"

"What? You think I am informer, maybe? You policemen are all the same. No, I don't know of anyone who wanted to kill Augustyn," Federenkov said heatedly.

"I will tell you this. No one liked him. No one. Not even MacKensie. The only reason that Augustyn was even here is because MacKensie needed the grant he brought to keep Station Alpha funded. Bah. Politics. That is not science. Do you have any more questions, or can I get to work?"

"I think that will be all for the moment, Dr. Federenkov," McKernan said calmly. "Thank you for your cooperation."

The Russian got up and left the room.

"A very passionate young man, our Dr. Federenkov," McKernan said after the door had closed.

"About his work," Ortiz commented. "And maybe Dr. Toranaga."

"But could he kill Augustyn?" McKernan queried. "I have my doubts. What about you, constable. Any observations?"

"No sir. Unless it's that Dr. MacKensie may have been playing a bit of a matchmaker."

McKernan smiled. "You think?"

INTERVIEW –
MOLLY MACDOUGAL
DAY 3, 11:00-11:30

Despite her name, Molly MacDougal, was a trim dark-haired Italian in her middle forties. It was evident that in her youth she would have had the looks of an Italian film star. Now she had taken on the appearance of a Madonna in a painting of one of the old masters with the serene beauty of one at peace with herself.

"You know that the Inspector and I are old friends," she said to Ortiz as she took her seat at the table.

"Oh?" Ortiz said taken by surprise.

"Yes, back when he first came to Mars. Let see. It must have been nearly six Earth years ago. He knew my husband, Jordy MacDougal quite well. The three of us spent quite a few nights drinking together at Finnegan's."

Finnegan's was Mars City's one real bar, where the beer was cold and the Scotch was real. It was owned and run by an Irishman named Finnegan. No one was quite sure what he was doing on Mars, but if they ever got around to holding an election for the mayor of Mars City, Finnegan would win hands down.

"That's a side of the Inspector I hadn't envisioned," Ortiz responded.

"Jordy was the pilot on the First Martian Science Expedition," McKernan explained. "That's the first one that Dr. MacKensie was chief scientist on. He came back as pilot for the Second and Third expeditions as well. He practically invented the art of flying on Mars single handed. When I came to Mars to take over as the head of security he was the one who checked me out in a Marsplane. I'd flown fighters and recon back on Earth, but flying on Mars is nothing like that. It takes a certain knack. Jordy was the best. Anyway, we became friends. There were fewer people on Mars back then, and you picked your friends if you were smart."

"Eric was still pretty green back then. But he learned quick," Molly commented.

"I haven't seen you in a while," McKernan said.

"Well, I've been here since the Station opened. Mac got me the job after, well, after Jordy died. I don't get much farther than Junction 3 these days."

"Jordy was a good man," McKernan said.

"One of the best."

"Well, I know you've got to get ready for lunch. I'll try to keep this brief."

"There's no rush. It's just soup and sandwiches. The sandwiches are made and the soup is on the stove."

"Could you tell us what you did the night before Dr. Augustyn's body was discovered?" McKernan asked.

"After dinner, I cleaned up as always and did the prep for the next day. The rumor was going around that the storm was going to break and they might be able to take the buggies out. I thought they'd be making an early start, so I got things ready for breakfast. I guess I went to bed a little later than usual, around 21:00 or 21:30. I think Sara Toranaga might already have been in her room and Sigrid and Nils came in a little later."

"You saw them?"

"Sure. They're a little old to sneak around. There are no secrets in a place like this."

"And they all stayed in the women's wing all night?"

"Well, I'm a heavy sleeper, but my room is right next to the airlock. I didn't hear the alarm go off during the night. I'm pretty sure I was the first one up at 06:00. I fixed breakfast for myself, and then started putting things out for the others. They started showing up about 07:00."

"And did you see Dr. MacKensie enter the lab wing?"

"Well, I saw him grab a cup of coffee about 07:00. He's always the first one up. I didn't see him enter the lock, but I heard the alarm right after he got the coffee. That must have been when he entered. The others came into the dining room between 07:00 and 07:30. It was a little after 07:30 when Mac came out and announced that Dr. Augustyn was dead."

"Was everyone in the dining room then?"

"I can't say for sure. Most of them were. I think Dieter and Sean may still have been in the men's wing. I was pretty busy cooking breakfast, so I didn't really look into the dining room. The serving counter is on the hall that leads to the airlock, so I mostly saw people as they got coffee or juice or grabbed a plate. But I'm pretty sure that everyone was there when Mac made the announcement. At least I don't remember noticing anyone missing."

"Well, I don't think it matters. What you've said pretty much agrees with everyone else's story. How did you get on with Dr. Augustyn?"

"I didn't," Molly said bluntly. "I tried not to have anything to do with him. He wasn't a nice man."

"Didn't he have oversight over you budget?"

"No. That was all separate through the Trust Authority. I reported directly to Dr. MacKensie. Dr. Augustyn complained about that once, but Mac told him to mind his own business. That kept him pretty quiet. Besides, he was only here for the season, while Mac, Jason and I are the permanent staff."

"Was there anyone that you know of who might have had a reason to kill Dr. Augustyn?"

She thought about that for a moment, as if considering whether to say anything.

"There was me."

"Are you saying that you killed Dr. Augustyn?" McKernan asked sharply.

"No. I'm saying that I had a reason to kill him. As to the others, well, you'll have to ask them. Dr. Augustyn was not someone that was liked."

"Would you care to explain?"

"Now that I've said it, I guess I had better," she said quietly.

"You know about how Jordy died, of course?"

"I ran the attempt to recover his body. I know he was flying out to pick up a bunch of V.I.P.s at one of the corporate camps so that they could make the ship back to Earth. That it was a flight that he probably shouldn't have made because of the weather."

"That's what Jordy said. He kind of ran Martian aviation back then, and he had grounded all the planes. All three of them back then I think. But these big wigs out at one of the camps made a big stink about how they were going to miss the ship back to Earth if someone didn't come to pick them up."

"Back then, there might be a gap of three or four months between ships," McKernan explained to Ortiz. "Perhaps more depending on how Mars and Earth were oriented."

"Jordy told them that if they were so concerned, they shouldn't have gone out to the camp in the first place. They went behind Jordy's back and arranged for Nelson to make the flight. Nelson worked for the mining company who's camp it was, and not for the Trust Authority, and basically they told him it would cost him his job if he didn't get them back to Mars City in time for the rocket. Nelson was good, but he wasn't as good as Jordy, and they both knew it. When Jordy found out he told Nelson that he'd make the flight in his place. So he did, and he was right, the weather was too bad for flying. He got caught in a down draft crossing a ridge and crashed."

Her voice caught at that and McKernan could see a tear forming in the corner of her eye.

"I'm sorry that we have to go over this, Molly," McKernan said. "Jordy was a good friend, and the best damned pilot on Mars. But why is this important?"

"One of the V.I.P.s that he was supposed to pick up was James Augustyn. He was the one who made a stink with the company so that they put pressure on Nelson. If it wasn't for him, nobody would have made that flight."

"I didn't know," McKernan said. "I was too busy with the rescue efforts. By the time that was over, they had all already gone back to Earth."

"Yeah. That's the thing. They made the ship back to Earth. Sure they had to spend four days in a buggy driving across Mars, but they made it with a day to spare. There had been no need for anyone to make that flight. No reason for Jordy to die."

"Mars was a dangerous place back then, Molly. It still is," McKernan said.

"Yes, I know. Jordy knew, too, better than anyone. But he loved it. I heard that Nelson died in a crash about a year later."

"Yeah," McKernan said flatly. "But I have my doubts that it was an accident. I've never been able to prove it, but I think the crash might have been tied into the Morrison affair."

"Nelson was a nice guy. He always treated me well. Especially after Jordy died. So, you see that I had more reason than most to want Augustyn dead."

"But you didn't do it, did you?" McKernan asked gently.

"No. It wouldn't bring Jordy back, would it? I loved that man. We had eight years together. I wouldn't trade those for the world. But I've made peace with myself. I have my memories."

"I think that will be all. Thanks Molly," McKernan said.

"Molly?" Ortiz asked. "I've got one question if you don't mind?"

"Sure. Go ahead. It seems to be the day for questions."

"On your file it lists you under a different name, and, well, Molly isn't very Italian."

"That was Jordy. We met in a bar in Rome. It was right after I graduated from nursing school. He'd just gotten back after the Second Mars Expedition. He was something of a hero and oh so handsome in his uniform. He was also very drunk. It was a noisy place and when we were introduced he couldn't get my name right. It's Mellisandra. He kept calling me Molly all night. But he managed to get my phone number somehow, and he called me the next day to ask me out. But I was still Molly to him. We were married three months later. And I'm still Molly after all these years and I wouldn't change that for anything. I really loved that guy."

"Thanks for telling me," Ortiz said. "I wish I could have met him."

"You would have liked him," Molly answered. "Well, I've got to get lunch ready.

"Thanks Molly," McKernan said as he stood up to show her out.

As Molly left the room, McKernan's phone beeped with the ringtone he reserved for official communications. It was the Martian Trust Authority governor Garcia-Gomez. Just what McKernan needed.

"McKernan here, Governor," he answered reluctantly.

There was a delay of nearly a second before he heard a response, one of the maddening features of long distance communications on Mars where all such calls had to be routed through communications satellites.

"McKernan, I was just calling to see what progress you've made." Like many people, the governor seemed to be shouting into his phone as if that would make the signal go faster.

"Not much so far, I'm afraid, sir."

"Oh? I'm disappointed, Inspector. You've had three days already." If you ignore the two days that it took me to get here, McKernan thought. "You realize how important this is, don't you, McKernan. Dr. Augustyn had a very high profile on Earth."

"Well, we've examined the crime scene. There's no question about it being a murder."

"You're sure about that? No chance that it was an accident or a suicide?" The governor sounded hopeful.

"Not unless Dr. Augustyn decided to kill himself by striking himself in the back of the head with a hammer, and that's not very likely, is it?"

"No, I guess not. Do you have a suspect, then?"

"Yes, twelve of them.   Eleven if you rule out Dr. MacKensie.   It turns out that Dr. Augustyn was not particularly well liked by his colleagues.   Everyone I've interviewed has at least some sort of grudge against him. He wasn't the nicest person, and he did have some ethical lapses in his past."

"That's not the kind of thing we want to let get around, Inspector," Gomez said.   "After all, Dr. Augustyn was the victim, not the criminal. And he had lots of highly placed friends."

"Not at Station Alpha, it would appear," McKernan said in response.   "Even Dr. MacKensie doesn't seem to have been too fond of him. I gather Dr. Augustyn's place at the station was against his wishes."

"Surely you can eliminate some of the suspects. After all, there are some very eminent scientists there."

"Oh, I can eliminate all of them.   As far as I can determine, everybody has an alibi. And so far I haven't been able to figure out how anyone could have gotten into the lab that night without being detected. But we're still working on it."

"I don't think I need to emphasize how sensitive this matter is, Inspector. It needs to come to a satisfactory conclusion and that needs to happen soon. And we can't afford any missteps, either.   No mistaken accusations. There are some very important people involved and nearly a dozen different governments."

"I fully understand that, Governor. That's why I'm trying to do a very thorough and careful job. One that can't be questioned after the fact."

"Yes, of course.   I'm sure you're handling this in a professional manner. Well let me know as soon as you have something." The call broke off.

McKernan sat there for a moment staring at his phone.

"Just what we need, a bloody politician. He wants us to solve the crime, but in a way that won't pin the crime on any of the suspects. And he wants it done yesterday."

"Isn't that the way it always is, sir," Ortiz said. McKernan just nodded.

"What do we do now, sir? Do you want me to get the next interviewee? Dieter Frederichson?"

"Yeah, might as well," McKernan said. "No, forget that. I've had enough of interviewing people for now. Let's break for lunch."

Mckernan and Ortiz had a quick lunch of a vegetable soup and bread, sitting apart at a table in the dining area. Neither talked much during lunch, but when they had finished Ortiz asked, "What do we do now? We've interviewed people and gone over the crime scene."

McKernan smiled, "I think it's time we to take a walk."

Ortiz just raised her eyebrows in response.

"The airlock records show no one used the airlock between the main building and the lab from the time Augustyn entered the lab at 24:12 and the time MacKensie entered at 07:02 the next morning. If the murderer didn't use that airlock, he, or she, must have gotten in or out of the lab another way. So I think we should take a look around the outside of the lab and the other buildings for signs of a forced entry."

"It's been three days since the murder. Do you think there will still be footprints?" Ortiz asked.

"Well, constable, we know it hasn't rained. Let's face it, even with the dust storm, the atmosphere is so thin that footprints will remain visible for a long time."

"Makes sense. I'm ready whenever you are, sir," Ortiz said shifting into professional mode.

On the way to the lab airlock they dropped off their soup bowls on the serving counter opening into the kitchen where they could see Molly cleaning up.

Chapter 10
Day 3, 13:00-21:00

As had happened the previous times they used the airlock an alarm sounded when the hatch opened. While not overpowering, it was certainly loud enough to have been heard throughout the main building and the lab.

While each of the modules that made up the station had its own airlock to the outside, the airlock at the far end of the lab building was the one most used. The reason for this was obvious. Next to the airlock were the lockers where all of the station's occupants stored their surface suits and a room for donning and removing the same. The previous night, MacKensie had pointed out two unused lockers where they had stowed their own suits.

Though Martians tended not to be prudes, McKernan noted that there was a partition in the locker room to provide at least some minimal level or privacy. Ortiz, he noticed was quick to take advantage.

He pulled his own suit out of the locker and began the pre-use check list. This was one thing no experienced Martian ever skipped or hurried, at least not the ones that survived. He had learned long ago to never rush this. From the other side he could hear Ortiz doing the same, quietly reciting the list of each point out loud with military precision, a holdover from her time in the Air Force. McKernan nodded approvingly. After all, his life might depend on how careful the constable was.

He stripped off his inside clothes and donned the tight-fitting long underwear that went under the suit itself. This layer provided both insulation and a smooth surface that the suit could slide over. Unlike a full space suit, surface suits were not completely pressurized. Though air-tight, they relied on their elasticity to maintain pressure on the extremities. This not only kept the weight of the suit down, but made them much more flexible than space armor, which used hard, articulated joints for mobility.

Getting into a suit was always a bit of a chore, almost like putting on a full body girdle. He could hear Ortiz grunting on the other side of the partition. He probably sounded the same to her. He squeezed his head up through the neck ring where the helmet was fastened and zipped up the front closure. The gloves attached separately and lace up boots went over the feet of the suit.

It was certainly possible to put on the backpack that provided life support by yourself, but it was much easier to have a partner do it for you. He let Ortiz attach the pack and couple the power and air connections to his neck ring, then did the same for the constable. When that was completed and the connections had been checked, they donned their helmets to the neck rings with a twist and click. Ortiz, he noted had a star stenciled on each side of her helmet. Surface suits were highly personalized items, and he had never insisted on any sort of official uniform policy. His own suit was a reddish tan that tended to blend in with most Martian landscapes, while the helmet was a plain black. A lot of the prospectors and surveyors had suits that ran to the fanciful and colorful.

They pressurized the helmets, and then went over the last part of the check list, to confirm air, power, and communications. He instructed Ortiz to switch over to a frequency reserved for law enforcement. They gave each other one more check of the backpack connections.

"Ready to go?"

"Ready when you are, sir."

He opened the inner hatch of the airlock and stepped through. Ortiz followed closing the hatch after her, latching it with the dogs provided. All the old science fiction movies to the contrary, most airlock doors on Mars were manual. There was less to go wrong.

There was a button to cycle the airlock. McKernan pressed it and they waited the 90 seconds it took to depressurize the chamber. When the cycle light changed to green, McKernan opened the latches on the outer door and they stepped outside.

He hadn't paid that much attention when they had arrived last night, but the airlock opened out onto a concrete pad about four meters square. It had been placed there in an effort to keep dust from being tracked inside, always a problem on Mars. There was a push broom leaning up against the side of the lab that showed plenty of use. So much for foot prints at this lock.

"I want to do a walk around of all of the buildings," McKernan said. "Let's start this way," he said pointing toward the left. "Keep your eyes open and let me know if you spot anything."

Walking in Mars gravity wasn't nearly as big a problem as walking on the moon, and after six years, McKernan didn't even noticed the special effort required. Ortiz hadn't been on Mars nearly as long, but she probably spent more of her time outside than McKernan and was even more sure footed.

The side of the lab was anything but smooth. In addition to a number of windows there were any number of electrical connections, cables to various external instruments and so on. About halfway down that side of the lab was a tower on which were mounted a number of antennas and dishes. It was about what McKernan had expected.

The dust and sand was only a few centimeters thick in this area. Presumably it had all been swept clean during construction and what there was had accumulated since. They walked slowly along the side until they came to the junction with the main building. There had been a few foot prints, but they looked fairly old.

The airlock between the two buildings was a smooth tube a little more than three meters tall. There were no breaks or hatches in its surface. Along the side of the main building, about where the store room for the kitchen was, there was another airlock, this one equipped with a docking tube. McKernan guessed that this was to facilitate unloading supplies. He made a mental note to check and see if this lock was monitored like the others. There were tire marks where a buggy had been backed up against the docking tube. None of the foot prints seemed newer.

"We'll have to find out when the last time supplies were delivered to this lock," he commented to Ortiz.

They kept walking around the station. The airlock between the administration building and the women's wing looked just like the one joining it to the lab. The outside of the women's wing was smoother than that of the lab. There were small windows for each of the rooms, and a larger group of windows at the end where there was a sort of lounge area. There didn't seem to have been any recent activity along this part of the complex.

There was another airlock at the end of the women's wing with another hard pad slightly smaller than the one by the lab. It didn't seem to get much use. If anyone had gone out that way it had been a long time ago.

As they got to the other side of the women's wing, they both caught their breath. They had looked out over the escarpment from inside the dining room, but seeing it on the outside was completely different. Between the building and the edge of the cliff there was about ten meters. From there the ground just dropped out of sight, and you could see out into the distance, farther than he'd ever seen on Mars before. McKernan had been to the Grand Canyon once as a kid. This wasn't as deep, nor as steep, but in its own way it was more impressive.

"MacKensie sure knows how to pick a view," McKernan said.

"It would be a great place to build a hotel," Ortiz joked.

They both stood there for a couple of minutes taking in the view. The dust storm had pretty much died down over the last day and the atmosphere had considerably cleared. They could see all the way to the pinkish sky on the horizon.

"Let's keep moving."

The escarpment side of the women's wing was very much a mirror image of the other side. It didn't seem like there had been much recent activity which McKernan found a little surprising considering the view. Maybe the scientists were a bit jaded and content just to look out the window.

The front side of the admin building was uninterrupted except for the string of windows on the library, conference and dining rooms. As they walked past the latter they could see David Chen and Antonio Berlanescu watching them from inside. As they passed by Chen gave them a wave.

The men's wing was constructed just like the women's wing except it was a little longer. There was another airlock at the end, but this one seemed to get a lot more traffic. It was easy to see why, as there was a path of foot prints leading toward a small promontory that jutted out from the escarpment. If there was any place to catch the view, this was it. Some of the footprints seemed recent, but they only led from the airlock to the outlook and back.

They kept circling the men's wing until they came back to where the admin building joined the lab without finding anything. There was another airlock/freight door on the admin building to match the one leading to the storeroom on the other side of the lock, but this didn't seem to have been used in the recent past.

They were half way down the lab building when Ortiz spotted something.

"Sir, take a look at this!"

There was a kind of access panel, about a meter and a half high and maybe forty centimeters wide. It would be a tight squeeze for someone in a surface suit, but a small person could probably manage it. The panel didn't fit quite flush and there were scratches on the fasteners as if it had been used recently.

Looking down, there were a set of foot prints in the dust. They weren't very distinct, but they were deep enough to be fairly recent. They didn't run along the side of the building, either, but headed almost perpendicularly away from it. Unfortunately, the ground on this side of the building had less dust and the trail petered out about ten meters from the lab. They separated, casting around trying to pick up the trail, but neither of them could spot anything.

"That's pretty interesting, sir," Ortiz said.

"Yeah. My thoughts, exactly. I wonder what's behind this panel. We'll have to look up the blueprints of the lab."

"No telling where the foot prints lead. They could go around to the airlock on the end of the men's wing."

"Maybe. The ground on this side of the buildings doesn't have much dust. I think they act like a wind break. Let's keep moving, and see if we spot anything else."

They completed their walk around the station, but nothing else caught their eye.

After they had gone back inside and changed out of their surface suits they went back to the conference room.

McKernan called up the station blueprints and displayed those of the lab building on the big video screen at the end of the room. It was clear enough where the panel was. There was a kind of chamber with a lot of piping and conduits. It looked kind of tangled, but there was also an access hatch on the inside of the lab.

"It just might be possible for someone to get through there if they were small and flexible enough."

"Without triggering the pressure sensors?" Ortiz asked.

"Maybe. The blueprints say that the access hatches on both the inside and outside are gasketed to hold pressure. If you opened the one on the outside, it wouldn't drop pressure in the lab. If you then closed it behind you and then opened the inside one slowly it might not be noticed. You could get out by reversing the process."

"Wouldn't that mean the chamber would still be at surface pressure?"

"Unless you came back and opened the inside hatch. It's been three days, and people have been in and out of the lab since then."

"It sounds complicated, sir," Ortiz stated. "Somebody would really have to know what they were doing. And be a contortionist. I'm not sure you could get through all that piping with a surface suit and a backpack on."

"Yeah, but you might not have to if you waited till the pressure equalized. And It still doesn't explain how you could get back in through one of the regular airlocks without the fact being recorded."

"So where does that leave us? Who would know enough how things work to do this?"

"Philips would be the logical choice. Unfortunately, all the people at this station are pretty bright. About the only people we could eliminate would be those that are too big to squeeze through the hatch."

They sat looking at the blueprint for a moment.

"Round up Philips. I want to open the inside hatch and see what it's like in there. And I want to see what his reaction is when I do it."

Ten minutes later they were in the lab with MacKensie and Philips. The maintenance man had his toolbox with him.

"Do you know what's on the other side of this hatch?" McKernan asked.

"It has something to do with the cooling systems, doesn't it Jason?" Dr. MacKensie asked.

"That and some of the gases used in the lab. There are a couple of transformers for the power feeds, too."

"When was the last time you were back there?" McKernan asked.

"I had to check on something last week. There was a gas leak. But I went in from the outside."

"But it is air-tight? You can open the hatch from this side without it decompressing us?"

"Should be able to. The way the panel is built, if there's no pressure on the inside, it will be real hard to open."

"Go ahead, then."

Philips worked on the fasteners for a minute or two, working methodically. He seemed unconcerned. When the last one was released, the panel pulled off easily. McKernan poked his flashlight through the opening. As the blueprint had showed, there was a tangle of plumbing and electrical conduits.

"Do you really think someone could have gotten through there?" MacKensie asked.

"I don't know. It's possible, maybe," McKernan responded. He flashed his light around some more, but there really wasn't anything to see.

"Is this panel or the one on the outside tied into the monitors?"

"No," Philips answered. "No reason. If there was a leak, the pressure sensors in the lab would alert us. I only need to get in there once or twice a year."

"OK. Thanks. You can button it up again."

Later, when they were back in the conference room Ortiz said, "Philips didn't seem to bat an eye. If he was hiding anything he's a pretty cool customer."

"Yeah, that was my impression, too. And MacKensie seemed pretty skeptical of the idea, too."

"So where does that leave us?"

"You got me."

CHAPTER 11
DAY 3, 21:00-22:00

McKernan was sitting at a table in the dining area sipping the dregs of a cup of coffee while he stared out the window at the Martian darkness. Ortiz had retired to the conference room to work over her notes of the day. The four card players were clustered around their usual table on the other side of the room engrossed in a game. The rest of the staff had scattered to the lab or their rooms.

Molly MacDougal walked up to the table with a coffee pot and a cup.

"Need a refill?"

"Sure," McKernan replied. Real coffee was rare enough on Mars that he never refused. He didn't care if it kept him awake and gave him indigestion.

She filled his cup, set down the one in her hand and filled that.

"Mind if I join you?" she asked.

"Please," he said indicating a seat on the other side of the table. "This is good coffee."

"Thanks," she said shyly. "I import the beans myself. Jordy's pension includes a shipping allowance. I mostly use it on coffee, olive oil, San Marzano tomatoes, salami, prosciutto, cheese. Life's too short not to have good food."

"You're in the wrong place then," Mckernan responded.

"I don't know. It's getting better. I can actually get some decent fresh vegetables from the farm at Junction 3 now. I grow my own basil and herbs. I know some people who are planning on making goat's milk cheese."

"Mind if I ask you a question?"

"Isn't that your job?"

"This is more of a personal one."

"Go ahead."

"Why are you still here? On Mars I mean. After Jordy died you could have gone home."

"Yeah, I could have gone back to Earth. Anglo-Martian was ready to send me back. Don't get me wrong, they were very nice about it. They were going to pay out the rest of my contract and there was Jordy's pension. I could have bought an apartment in Rome or someplace."

"But you didn't go back."

"No. When it came down to it, there wasn't anything left for me there. My father died when I was a kid, my mother died from cancer the first year I was on Mars. My sister had moved to Palermo, and I never did get along with her, anyway. Maybe it would have been different if I had grown up out in the country in some little village, but I grew up in the slums of Rome. I don't know if you can understand what that was like?"

"I can guess. I grew up in one of the less desirable parts of L.A."

"Anyway, there didn't seem to be any reason to hurry back to Earth. Anglo-Martian was happy enough for me to complete my contract. Medical personnel were at a premium back then. Still are, for that matter. I could have gone home when the contract expired but then Mac offered me a job as nurse/cook on one of his expeditions into the back country. I discovered that I liked feeding scientists. They're mostly good people. A bit focused on their work, but if you feed them right they appreciate it. It helped me get over Jordy's death. That led to this job when Station Alpha opened. I've been on Mars eight years, now. I know a lot of good people that I like. On Earth, I've got nothing."

McKernan shrugged.

"Why the interest?"

"I don't know. I guess I've been thinking a lot about it lately. Going back to Earth. My second three year contract is coming up soon. I'm trying to decide whether to sign a third. I've also got the chance to buy the hut next to mine in Hut Town at a bargain rate. I could put together a pretty nice place. Lots of room. But it would only make sense if I stick around."

"You'll stay," Molly observed.

"You think?"

"I've seen that look in others. The old timers. There comes a point where there's more for them on Mars than there is back on Earth. A chance to build something rather than just survive. A future to look forward to. You've been here, what, five years. Even in that time things have gotten better, more settled, more comfortable. You can't say the same about Earth."

They sat in silence looking out the window. The lights in the dining area had been turned down low so that they could see some of the brighter stars. The surface was pitch black. There weren't any settlements or prospectors within view. A bright light moved slowly across the sky. Phobos or maybe the docking station in low orbit. McKernan wasn't sure which.

"Do you ever have regrets?"

"About what? Coming to Mars? Marrying Jordy? Not a minute of it. I loved that man. The eight years we had together were the happiest of my life. The only bad time was the year he was on Mars with the Third Scientific Expedition when I was left behind on Earth. That's why I jumped at the chance to come to Mars when he took the job with Anglo-Martian. We'd be together. That was all that mattered."

Molly took a sip of her coffee. "They never recovered the body, you know. It might have made a difference."

"I know. I flew over the crash site during the investigation. It's real rough country. Nowhere to land within twenty kilometers. There wasn't much left to salvage, either, just junks of metal scattered over five hectares of rock outcrops. He never had a chance. If I could have found a place to land, I would have."

"I know. I don't blame you. Nelson said the same thing."

"I've got a bit of grappa in the kitchen. We could make a toast to Jordy and all the others out there," she said with a wave of her hand.

"I'd be proud to," McKernan answered.

She returned a few minutes later with a bottle and two small glasses. She poured the clear liquid into the glasses and passed him one. "To Jordy."

"To Jordy, and Nelson, and all the others."

The grappa burned on the way down, but it was good. Certainly better than any of the local hootch. They sat staring at their drinks for a while in silence.

"So who do you think killed Augustyn?" McKernan asked after a while.

"Back to playing the cop again?" Molly said with a smile.

"Always."

"I just don't know," she said thoughtfully. "Augustyn was a pain, a real ass-hole. He rode anybody he could away with it. But I just can't see any of them killing him. Sigrid, Nils and Breaker are all pretty well made in their careers. Augustyn just didn't carry enough weight to cause them real problems. Those guys over there," she said gesturing at the card players, "they're all young, full of themselves, and think they're immortal. They thought of Augustyn more as a joke, someone to get around, not as a real threat."

"What about Toranaga and Federenkov?"

"I can't see them doing it either. Toranaga is too smart. If she wanted to get at Augustyn, she'd find a better way, something not lethal. And it's not like Boris had anything to be jealous about. Sarah loathed Augustyn. She said he gave her the creeps. I could see Boris punching him in the nose, but nothing more."

"So that leaves you, Philips and MacKensie."

"You are playing the copper. You don't have to believe it, but I didn't kill Augustyn, and you can't think Mac did it. After Jordy, he's the best man I've ever known."

"That leaves Philips," McKernan said.

"I just don't see it that way. I know him better than most because I'm one of the help. I know he had a rough time on Earth, but he's really a nice guy."

"So no one did it?"

"You asked my opinion. I just can't think that any one of them could commit cold blooded murder."

"You're a big help. That leaves me either with Martians that can walk through walls or Augustyn killed himself."

"That would make it easier, wouldn't it?" Molly asked.

"Yeah it would. Well, it's getting late. I think I'll call it a night. Thanks for the coffee and the grappa."

"Any time, Inspector."

CHAPTER 12
DAY 3, 22:00-22:30

On his way to the men's wing McKernan passed the table of card players. Tonight it appeared they were playing poker.

"Care to sit in for a hand, Inspector?" David Chen asked as he walked by.

"No, I think I'll just kibitz for a bit. It's getting late."

"Our loss. We could use some fresh stakes. As it is we just pass the same money around amongst us."

"You play for money?" McKernan asked.

"Yeah, Martian rials. Dieter's the winner this week. I think he's up about a thousand or so." They all laughed. The official currency on Mars was U.N. script issued in dollar denominations. The term Martian "rial" was used when a person wanted to indicate something was worthless, as in "not worth a Martian rial." Some enterprising soul with access to a printer had printed up a bunch of bills in various denominations of rials for sale to tourists and newcomers until he had been shut down. The few surviving bills had become collector's items.

"So you play most nights."

"Not much else to do," Dieter Frederichson said.

"Don't get us wrong," Chen explained. "We all work hard when we can. But you can't work sixteen hours a day, not and keep sharp. You can only read so many books or watch so many bad videos. And the delightful Toranaga only has eyes for Boris, the lucky dog. That only leaves the Ice Queen and Mom in the feminine department. So we play cards. Poker tonight, pinochle tomorrow, bridge on Fridays, and so on."

"The Ice Queen and Mom?" McKernan queried.

"Dr. Oddsdottir and Mrs. McDougal. The good doctor is a bit old for us young bucks and besides, she has Nils when she feels the need. As for Molly, she takes care of us, feeds us, makes sure we wear our scarves and galoshes when we go outside. No one would dare to make improper advances to Ms. Molly. That, and I think she's a one man woman, and she's still in love with the late Mr. McDougal."

McKernan had come to the conclusion that David Chen had appointed himself class clown. Ever since that first meeting he'd been trying to think who he reminded him of. It had finally come to him, the actor who had played the number two son in an old Charlie Chan movie.

Chen lost the next hand trying to bluff with a pair of sevens.

"So, Inspector, have you figured out who put the ax in our late den leader?"

"Not yet. Everybody seems to have had a motive and no one had an opportunity."

"That's harsh," Chen responded.

"I find it hard to think that any one of us could have killed him," Antonio Berlanescu said.

"But the inspector is right, Tony. All of us did have motives to kill him, if being a prick is grounds for murder. Let's face it. With everybody cooped up the last couple of weeks because of the storm, it doesn't take too much imagination to see someone going over the edge and dropping an ax in Jimmy's skull. The question is, who?"

"So who do you suspect, Dr. Chen?" McKernan asked sarcastically.

"Please, call me David. We're all friends here. Who do I suspect? Well let's see. I think the four of us can be excluded. We all provide alibis for each other most of the night. By the way, have you figured out exactly when the good doctor was offed?"

"No, unfortunately, Dr. MacKensie, in trying to keep the crime scene intact, made it impossible to judge the time of death from the body. By the time we got here to examine the body, it was stone cold. Not that anything else could have been done. Even Ortiz was eight hours away, but someone might have been able to take the temperature of the body or note if rigor had set in. All we really know is that the murder occurred sometime between midnight when he entered the lab and when Dr. MacKensie discovered the body in the morning."

"Bad luck for you, then, Inspector. Where was I. Well, if you rule out the four of us, who does that leave. There's the Ice Queen, I know she hated his guts in a dispassionate way, and she does have Viking ancestors, but if she had wanted to take on Augustyn, she would have destroyed him professionally rather than physically. She could have done it, too. I would rule her out."

"Then there's our melancholy Dane, Dr. Jensen. Except he's too much of a modern Scandinavian and not all that melancholy. I know Augustyn had an affair with his wife, but from what I've heard, old Nils wasn't that unhappy to see her go."

"So what about our token Aussie, Breaker?" Chen asked.

Sean Moran spoke up for the first time. "It's a pretty open secret that Augustyn pinched some of his early work. It doesn't seem to have hurt his career, though. If he had really held a grudge I think he would have done something years ago. He'd have smacked him in the head with a beer mug at some faculty party."

"So how about the ravishing Toranaga or Boris the boy friend?" Chen queried.

"Boris might have done it to defend Sarah's honor," Dieter stated.

"Challenge him to a duel, maybe," Chen responded. "Ice axes at ten paces. Or more likely a deadly game of chess. Boris is a good guy and a genius, but he's not the physical type. Don't get me wrong. I think those two are in love, and each would risk death for the other if they felt they were really being threatened. But I don't think Augustyn had anything to touch them. I know Sarah has got a tenured position lined up. And Boris can probably go anywhere he wants. No, I think I'd rule those two out."

"So that leaves us only with the staff, Mom and Jason Philips. I personally can't see Mrs. MacDougal murdering anyone. She's far too maternal and angelic in my view. Jason, on the other hand—"

"He's kind of a strange one," Sean Moran continued. "Quiet like, never really tries to fit in. Maybe it's just that the rest of us are PhD's and all. Still, they always say you've got to watch out for the quiet ones."

"And he would be the obvious suspect to sabotage the alarms," Dieter chimed in. "After all he is the one responsible for maintaining them."

"I'd say that makes him the logical prime suspect," Chen commented.

"But what about motive?" Tony queried.

"Well, Augustyn did make his life hell. Always complaining about his work and rejecting requisitions and paperwork," Chen countered.

"But is that enough to kill someone over. He just doesn't seem the type. Not volatile enough," Tony stated.

"So speaks our temperamental Latin type."

There was a moment of silence, then McKernan spoke. "I notice there is one person you didn't mention."

"There is? Oh, yes. Dr. MacKensie. Well, we can certainly rule him out. After all, he's the one who discovered the body. I also can't even contemplate Mac committing evil. The man's a saint. A legend. No, I think we'll have to look elsewhere than our fearless leader."

McKernan found himself smiling in spite of himself. He also found that Chen's analysis was surprisingly close to his own.

"Have we been of help, Inspector?" Tony asked.

"It's been very enlightening, gentlemen. You've been quite helpful. But I think it's time I head off to bed. Good night."

INTERVIEW – DAVID CHEN
DAY 4, 08:30-08:45

"Well, let's get the rest of the interviews out of the way," McKernan said to Constable Ortiz as they set up in the conference room on the fourth day since the murder. "I've scheduled Dr. Chen, Dr. Berlanescu, Dr. Frederichson and Dr. Moran up first. I'm not expecting anything new that we didn't get from the others, but you never know. We have to go through the motions in any case."

If there was little doubt by his face of David Chen's Chinese ancestry, the fact that for the last several centuries his ancestors had lived in California was just as apparent in his body and manner. Certainly at 180 centimeters and 80 kilos he looked as though he would be much more at home on a tennis court than in a rice paddy. And while his ancestors may have at one time built railroads, his more immediate predecessors owned them, or at least substantial portions thereof. While it was quite possible that he and the inspector had been born within fifty kilometers of each other they had grown up in completely different worlds. David Chen was completely comfortable with whom he was.

"Inspector, Constable," Chen said as he took a seat at the table. "I'm sorry if my remarks earlier offended you. This is a novel situation for me. I've never been a suspect in a murder before."

"I understand, Dr. Chen. Let's get down to business. I just have a few questions about what you did the night that Dr. Augustyn died."

"Where do you want me to start?"

"Why don't you start immediately after dinner. I assume you had dinner with the others at the usual time?"

"Yes. I sat with Tony, Dieter and Sean. We usually do. Boris and Sarah sat together, as usual, and Roger, Nils, Dr. Oddsdottir, and Mac sat at another table."

"What about Dr. Augustyn and Jason Philips?" McKernan asked.

"They sat alone. No one really liked to eat with Dr. Augustyn if they could avoid it and Philips always kept to himself. So it was the youngsters, the elders, the loving couple and two singles. Molly stayed in the kitchen."

"What happened then?"

"After dinner I think Nils and Sigrid watched a video before discretely retiring. Boris said he had a paper or something to work on. Mac went into the lab. I think he had some paperwork to take care of. Roger hung around for a while, then went into the men's wing. Sarah went to the women's wing at some point, I'm not quite sure when. I try--, tried not to pay too much attention to Dr. Augustyn, so I'm not quite sure what he was doing. The rest of us, Tony, Dieter, and Sean ended up playing cards. We do that most nights. Not much else to do except work, and with this dust storm, we've had plenty of time to work on reports and things during the day."

"What about Philips? Do you know what he was doing?"

"Sorry. Like I said, he keeps to himself. Doesn't mix much. He's a nice enough guy. Helpful, but I think he feels overwhelmed with all the Ph. D.s. I don't remember seeing him at all after dinner, so I guess he must have gone to his room."

"So you played cards?"

"Yes, pinochle, if I remember right."

"Until around 02:00? That's a long time to play cards," McKernan stated.

"Well, we don't take it too seriously and there's a lot of joking and talking shop and stuff. Usually we break up around midnight, but Dr. Augustyn got on our case about staying up late as if we were a bunch of school boys. I think it pissed us all off and we continued playing cards for another couple of hours just to spite him." Chen said the last in a flat, matter of fact tone.

"This was around midnight?"

"Somewhere around them. Mac, Dr. MacKensie came out of the lab at 24:00. I remember glancing at the clock as the alarm sounded on the air lock door. Augustyn came through a few minutes later, well maybe ten. I didn't pay too much attention. I didn't know then that he was going to get a hammer in his head due to a person or persons unknown."

"I take it you didn't like Dr. Augustyn," McKernan commented.

"Lord, no. Not to speak ill of the dead, but the guy was a real asshole. He was always giving a people a hard time if he could get away with it. I think he was a pathological bully. He couldn't pull stuff with Mac, or even Roger or Nils, and dear Sigrid would have eaten him for lunch if he dared cross her, but the rest of us he was always threatening to "write reports" or see about taking our grant money away for the stupidest things. I know he went on for days about Tony borrowing a hammer from the stock room when he misplaced his own. Like we'd ever miss it. The things are laying around all over the place. Everyone brings one and no one takes the bloody things home."

"Was there some one person that he picked on specifically?"

"Well, he didn't like Tony and he didn't like Sean, he really didn't like me, but then he found out who my father was and he backed off a little, but the guy I really felt sorry for was Philips. Anything that went missing, or broke, or didn't have the proper paperwork and it was always his fault. I know he's a queer duck, quiet and all, but he basically keeps this whole place running single handed. But he seemed to be really afraid of Augustyn for some reason. I never could figure out why."

"So what did you and the others do about Augustyn?"

"Mostly just blew him off. It's not like he could really do anything to us. We're all up for tenured positions when we get back. I know that Augustyn was supposed to be in line for some big position as the head of some institute or other, but so what. Besides, who wants to be an administrator. He might have been good at politics, but as a scientist, Dr. Augustyn was definitely second rate. The rumor is that even his first few papers, the ones that made his reputation, what there is of it, were based on stuff that he stole. And we wouldn't be here if we weren't the fair haired boys in our respective fields. With a season's experience on Mars any one of us can practically name his own ticket. Besides, we've got Mac behind us. And trust me, he carries a lot more weight than Augustyn ever did."

"Dr. MacKensie?"

"Why do you think we're here. Mostly because Dr. MacKensie read a paper or a thesis that we wrote and saw our 'potential.' This is kind of like a special session for people that he's taken a special liking to. Every one of us was handpicked except for Roger, Sigrid and Nils who are old friends and colleagues. And let's face it. Mac is Martian geology for all practical purposes. He's the grand old man. Here since the beginning."

"Did he often bring people in whom he had a special interest to Mars?" McKernan asked.

Chen reflected for a moment. "Now that you mention it, no. I mean he's always had an eye for bright young talent and managed places for them on expeditions. Roger can tell you about that. But normally just one or two at a time. It's odd, the six of us, because you have to include Sarah and Boris as fresh talent, being here in what is really kind of the off season. Usually the place fills up for about eight months during the Martian summer, which is why it's so big, but then pretty much closes down the rest of the year. And Sigrid, Nils and Roger are just here to show us the ropes. It's almost like Mac was looking for replacements for the old guard."

Chen got silent for a moment as if he was chewing things over. McKernan wondered what he was thinking about.

"You haven't said anything about Mrs. MacDougal," McKernan finally interrupted.

"The Madonna of the kitchen?" Chen quipped brightly, his train of thought broken. "She is a dear. Looks after all us young ones. She mostly ignored Dr. Augustyn, though I detected a real chill between them."

"But, if you say, Dr. Augustyn liked to bully people in subordinate positions--?"

"Augustyn wasn't stupid. He knew that there were some lines that he could not cross, and our Molly was one of them. Mac would have had a fit. Kicked him out the nearest airlock without a surface suit. No, Dr. Augustyn never gave Molly a hard time."

"Do you think there is anything between them, Molly and Dr. MacKensie I mean?"

"Lord, no. Perish the thought. But they do go back a long way. Molly's husband was the pilot on the First

Martian Science Expedition and Mac was the geologist. They were both on the Second Expedition, the one that Mac was chief scientist on, as well. I think it's just that Mac feels an obligation to look after her. It's the kind of think he'd do."

"Everybody I've talked to seems to say the same thing," McKernan commented. "He seems to have helped out everyone involved with this case, except maybe for Dr. Augustyn."

"Well, that's Mac for you," Chen agreed.

"Well, I won't take up any more of your time just now. Thank you, Dr. Chen. You've given me a lot to think over. If you think of anything else that might help, please let me know."

INTERVIEW –
ANTONIO BERLANESCU
DAY 4, 08:45-09:00

Dr. Antonio Berlanescu was the next to be interviewed. He was a tall northern Italian, around thirty, and handsome in a kind of a fleshy way that put McKernan in mind of a gigolo at some Mediterranean resort. The fact that he was on Mars, though, proved that there were some real brains behind the slightly vapid smile.

"Ciao," he said as he took a seat without being asked. "You wanted to ask some questions?" His English was fluent but accented. McKernan assumed that women back on Earth would find it charming. For no reason, he found that fact annoying.

"Thank you for sparing us the time, Dr. Berlanescu," McKernan replied. "I'm just trying to clarify where everyone was and what they were doing during the twelve hours or so before Dr. Augustyn's body was discovered."

"Sure. Well I had dinner like usual. Then I played cards with David Chen, Dieter, and Sean. Also like usual. I think it was pinochle night. I went to bed. Late. After 02:00. I didn't get up until 08:00. By that time Dr. MacKensie had already discovered the body."

"Do you always play cards that late?"

"No. Not when we're working. But the weather had been bad for over a week so we couldn't take the buggies out. There's not much else to do except play cards."

"Did you see anyone enter or leave the laboratory building?"

"Yeah. About 24:00 Dr. MacKensie came out of the lab. He came over to the table and said good night. He mentioned that it looked like the weather might be clearing.

Then he went into the men's wing. A few minutes later Dr. Augustyn went the other way. He told us to go to bed. I think that's why we stayed up so late. Normally we knock off around midnight. You know that's something I never understand. Is midnight 24:00 or forty minutes later at 00:00?"

"I think it's a matter of personal preference," McKernan responded. "And no one else entered the lab?"

"Not while we were playing cards. The lock is in clear view, and with the alarm sounding I don't think we could miss anyone. After 02:00 or so, I can't say."

"Is it possible that anyone was still in the lab when Dr. MacKensie came out?"

"I'm not sure. Well the four of us were playing cards. We could hear Molly in the kitchen until she went to bed. I know I saw Breaker and Boris go to the men's wing. Let's see. I think I remember Sarah going to her room early in the evening, 20:00 or so. Nils and Dr. Oddsdottir watched a video in the lounge and then snuck off to the women's wing after. That's pretty much everyone. OK, I'm not sure about Philips. I don't remember what he did after dinner."

"That's very helpful," McKernan said. "After Dr. Augustyn entered the lab, none of the other players got up?"

"What, like one of us got up to go to the bathroom, entered the lab without the alarm going off, whacked Augustyn on the back of the head, and then came back before the next hand?"

"Something like that," McKernan said. It did sound a little ridiculous.

"No. They were all in plain sight all of the time until the game broke up. I think Dieter and Sean went to bed a few minutes before David and me. We stayed up talking about what our plans were going to be when the dust storm broke. We wanted to go out to the same area to collect samples and plant some instruments."

"So you went to bed a little after 02:00. Did you hear anyone move around in the night?"

"Yeah. I think I heard Philips get up to go to the bathroom around 03:00. His room is at the end of the corridor, so he has to pass mine to get to the bathroom. None of the others do except for Dr. MacKensie. He's got the big room at the end. I think I heard him a bit later. I can't say when. Then people started getting up around 07:00 or so. I can't say exactly who or when."

There didn't seem to be much point in following that line of questioning any further.

McKernan pointed to an evidence bag on the table holding the murder weapon. "Do you know what this is?"

"Sure. It's a geologists hammer. Everybody here has one. Is that what was used to kill Dr. Augustyn?"

"Yes. Have you ever seen this particular hammer before."

Berlanescu looked it over.

"Sure. I borrowed it from the stock room."

"When was this?"

"A few weeks ago. Before the storm. I'd left my own hammer in one of the buggies the night before. We had a lot of samples to unload and I just forgot it. Dave Chen drove off in that buggy the next day before I had a chance to retrieve it, so I went to the stock room. There is a whole bin of the things there. Everybody brings a hammer to Mars, but no one wants to pay to ship them back. There must be a couple of dozen in the bin. I asked Philips if I could take one for the day. He said 'Sure, no problem.' So I grabbed the one on top. That one. I recognize it because of the initials on the handle."

"What happened to it? Did you keep it?"

"No.   When I got back from that days excursion Dr. Augustyn met me in the locker room.   He said that I had taken property without authorization.   What a pain, man. He said he was going to write up a report.   Like I was some kind of kid trying to steal it or something.   He was always doing stuff like that.   Threatening people.   I don't need that kind of shit.   I'm an adult.   I've got a professorship waiting at the University of Milan when I get back to Earth.   I let him take the stupid hammer.   Besides, Chen had brought mine in from the buggy.   He was in the locker room at the same time.   Saw the whole thing.   Ask him."

"We will.   So Dr. Augustyn took the hammer.   Did you see what he did with it?"

"Yeah.   I think he took it to his office and put it on a shelf.   At least I saw it there a few days later.   I don't think he ever took it back to the stock room."

That seemed to resolve that.

"Well, thank you, Dr. Berlanescu.   I think that's all the questions I have for now."

"Ciao."   The Italian got up to leave, the same vapid smile on his face that he had on when he had entered.

INTERVIEW –
DIETER FREDERICHSON
DAY 4, 09:00-09:15

Dr. Dieter Frederichson looked every bit the northern European. With his short blonde hair, chiseled features, and lean athletic body it would be easy to envision him as a storm-trooper or rocket engineer at Peenemunde in an earlier age. It was apparent that he tried to emulate the style of his card playing cohorts, but a certain Germanic stiffness kept him from pulling it off. One could never imagine his hair assuming the casual ruffled look of Tony Berlanescu.

"Good morning," he said as he sat down. His English, while accented, was precise and formal. "You have some questions you wish to ask about Dr. Augustyn?"

"Yes," McKernan replied. "I'd just like you to go over what you did from the evening before until the time that the body was discovered."

"I had dinner, as usual. Then I played cards with David, Tony, and Sean. We played until 02:00, when I went to bed. Sean went to bed at the same time. David and Tony stayed up a few minutes before coming to bed. I brushed my teeth and went to bed. I am a good sleeper, so I heard nothing until the alarm went off at 07:30 to wake me. I got up, washed, dressed and went into the dining room. This was about the time that Dr. MacKensie came in from the Laboratory Building to announce that Dr. Augustyn was dead."

"While you were playing cards, did you observe anyone entering or leaving the lab wing?"

"Yes. I was sitting at the table facing the airlock door. I had a clear view, and could not have missed anyone coming in and out, even if the airlock alarm hadn't sounded, which it did. Dr. MacKensie came out of the lab at 24:00. I noted the clock, which as you know is right above the airlock. He came over to the table, made some conversation, and then entered the Men's Dormitory Wing. A few minutes later Dr. Augustyn came out of the Men's Wing. He came over to the table and said that we should go to bed so we would be ready to work the next day if the dust storm had abated. Then he went through the airlock into the Laboratory Building at 24:12."

"And as far as you know, no one else was in the laboratory building?"

"I do not think so. As far as I can remember, everyone other than Dr. Augustyn and the four of us had gone to bed. The table we play cards at has a good view of all three airlocks, and, of course, the alarm sounds every time the airlocks are used."

"And you are sure of this?"

"Yes. I remember Dr. Morand and Dr. Toranaga going to their respective wings soon after dinner. Drs. Jensen and Oddsdottir watched a video and then went to bed, together, I assume, as they both went into the Women's Dormitory. Mrs. MacDougal went to bed after she had cleaned the kitchen and prepared for breakfast. She asked if we needed anything before she retired. She is a very nice lady. Dr. MacKensie I have already mentioned."

McKernan smiled. "What about Jason Philips? Where was he?"

Dr. Frederichson thought for a moment, a puzzled look on his face. "I do not remember. He was at dinner. Then he wasn't in the lounge area later. I do not remember him leaving. It may have been while we were taking our plates back to the kitchen after dinner and getting set up to play cards. I'm sorry. Philips is just not a memorable man."

"That interests me," McKernan said. "What is your opinion of Philips."

"He is a hard worker, very good at his job. Efficient. Personally, he is very quiet. He never mixes in. The only people who ever seemed to talk to him except for work were Dr. MacKensie and Mrs. MacDougal. And of course, Dr. Augustyn."

"Oh?"

"Yes. But not in a nice way. He was always complaining to him about his work, usually in public. And there was no need. As I said, Philips was very good at his job. I never had any complaint with either his work or his manner. I do not think any of the others did. There was one time Dr. Augustyn made a big fuss about a geologist's hammer. It was quite unnecessary."

"Tell me about it."

"Tony had left his hammer in one of the buggies the night before. He had had his hands full with some samples and didn't want to make a trip outside just to get the hammer. In the morning David and Dr. Morand had taken that buggy before Tony could get it. He and I were going out to collect more samples, so he went to the stockroom and asked Philips if he could take one of the extras. There is a big box of them right inside the stockroom door that have been left by previous expeditions. No one wants to pay to ship them back to earth. Philips said to just take one, so Tony did. When we returned from our excursion outside Dr. Augustyn was waiting and made a big fuss about it not being signed out. He said he was going to write up Tony and Philips, too. It was ridiculous. The damned hammer didn't even really belong to Station Alpha in the first place. It was just something that was left."

"Do you know what became of the hammer?"

"Dr. Augustyn grabbed it out of Tony's hand and took it back to his office. Like it was evidence. I don't know what happened to it afterwards."

"Did incidents like that happen often?"

"Yes. But only with David, Tony, Sean, Sarah, Boris, and me. Dr. Augustyn knew not to be unpleasant with Dr. Morand and Dr. Jensen. I also think he was a little afraid of Dr. Oddsdottir."

"Any particular reason?" McKernan asked.

"I'm not sure. I think something had happened in the past. But Dr. Oddsdottir is not someone that you cross. She is a very strong minded woman."

"Is there anything else you can tell me?" McKernan asked.

"No. Not that I can think of. What I have told you agrees with what the others have said?"

"Yes," McKernan replied. "Complete agreement. A surprising amount, actually."

"Not so surprising, I would think. We are all scientists, and scientists are very observant people."

"Yes, that's probably it," McKernan agreed. "Well, thank you. If you could ask Dr. Moran in."

"Good day," Dr. Frederichson said with a just perceptible nod and he got up and left the room.

Ortiz looked at her boss. "Do you think they cooked their stories?"

"Well, it's either that, or everyone is telling things exactly as they happened. How often does a policeman run into that? Even if no one is lying."

INTERVIEW – SEAN MORAN
DAY 4, 08:45-09:00

"Thank you for agreeing to answer a few questions, Dr. Moran," McKernan said. "I'll try to keep it brief."

"Sure. Whatever I can do to help clear up this thing."

Dr. Moran did not conform to the typical stereotype of the red-haired ruddy cheeked Irishman. He was slender and dark haired with a complexion that was pale rather than fair. He looked more like a poet than a scientist. Coming from the west of the Irish Republic, one of the areas where they still spoke Gaelic, his English was even more heavily accented than that of Dr. Frederichson. McKernan wondered if they could actually understand each other when they spoke.

"I'll try to keep this simple. You were playing cards with Dr. Chen, Dr. Berlanescu, and Dr. Frederichson from after dinner until around 02:00."

"Yeah. That's roight."

"Around 24:00 Dr. MacKensie left the lab wing and went to the men's wing, stopping to say a few words. A few minutes later, Dr. Augustyn went in the opposite direction."

"Yeah."

"As far as you know, no one else was in the lab wing from the time Dr. Augustyn entered until you went to bed?"

"Roight again. This is simple."

"After you went to bed, did you hear anything?"

"Tony and Chen came in maybe fifteen minutes after I did. Breaker told 'em to keep it down. It was late and I fell asleep pretty quick after that. Didn't hear anything until I got up around 07:30. By then everybody was moving around, getting up, taking showers and such."

"Could anyone have left the men's wing during the night?"

"They could have. Like I said, I was sleeping pretty good. But the bloody alarm goes off every time someone cycles the airlock. Someone would have heard it. I heard it when Dr. MacKensie used it around 07:00. That's what woke me up. It's not that loud, but it does get your attention. There's not much in the way of sound proofing, either, as I'm sure you know. Tony snores something awful."

McKernan smiled. The Italian did snore. Loudly.

"What was your opinion of Dr. Augustyn."

"If you want my personal opinion, he was a fookin' asshole. He was a bully whenever he thought he could get away with it. Always tryin' to make out with the girls, too. Or at least Sarah Toranaga, whose really the only girl here. I've heard rumors that he tried something once with Sigrid when they were younger and she shut him down pretty rudely. He hasn't tried that again. At least not here. Don't think Mac would put up with it either."

"So you didn't like him?"

"No. Nobody did. He was a bloody poser. A politician. He was good at getting grants and appointments and that sort of thing, but as a scientist he stunk. He only wrote one decent paper in his career, and I found out later that it was based on material he stole from Breaker Morand. The only things he's done in the last dozen years has been to put his name as coauthor on the work of a bunch of his grad students and post docs. Any one of the others here could run rings around him, especially Boris and Sigrid."

"Well Dr. Morand has got his television shows. Do you consider him a good scientist?"

"Sure. I like his tele stuff. Very entertaining, but sound. He still does good work. He basically wrote the book on volcanic ice flows. Fact is he did. Bloody good book.

Volcanic Ice Flows. He still comes out with a couple of decent papers a year despite the television and other stuff."

"Do you think he holds a grudge against Dr. Augustyn for stealing his research?"

"Breaker. Nah. If he did, he'd have wrapped a beer mug up the side of his head long ago. No, I don't think he sees the point. It's not like his career hasn't done well. And he's rollin' in money from the tele business and books and stuff. Man he's a celebrity. No one outside of the field has ever heard of Dr. Augustyn, and those that have, know what kind of a wanker he is."

"Do you know of anyone else that might have had a reason to kill Dr. Augustyn?"

"Well, if I was a bettin' man, I'd put my money on Philips. Augustyn seemed to have something over him. But I'd guess that if Jason wanted to do away with Augustyn he would have found a much cleverer way to do it. He's a smart lad, and really good with his hands. I'd think that he could find a way to fix it so you'd never know. Still, I don't think he did it. He's too quiet."

"The quiet ones often are the most dangerous," McKernan remarked.

"Sorry, I just don't see it. I feel sorry for him. Like I said, he's really good at fixing things and keeping them running, but he's stuck in an out of the way place like this. But if he went back to Earth, he probably couldn't even find a job. Not without the proper degrees and certifications. He's lucky that Dr. MacKensie took an interest in him and got him his job here."

"He seems to have done that a lot. Helping people out, that is."

"Yeah. He got me a grant to make this trip after reading a paper I wrote on methane phase shift on Titan during volcanic eruptions. Of course, Breaker liked it, too, which means a lot coming from him. I can e-mail you a copy?"

"I'm afraid I've got a full schedule at the moment, but thanks all the same," McKernan answered. He could see Ortiz smiling as she studiously checked the recorder.

"Well, I think you've pretty much confirmed what the others have told us. Is there anything else you'd like to tell us?"

"No. Sorry. I would if I could. I'd hate to have something like this hanging over Dr. MacKensie and Station Alpha. It's hard enough getting funding these days without having a scandal to deal with."

"Thanks then, I'll let you get back to work now."

INTERVIEW – JASON PHILIPS
DAY 4, 09:30-10:30

Jason Philips entered the conference room nervously. McKernan had the impression that this was not the first time he had been interviewed by the police, and that the experience had not been pleasant. This didn't particularly concern the inspector. He knew from Phillip's file that he had grown up in one of the poorer sections of L.A., not far, in fact, from the neighborhood that McKernan, himself, had been raised in. He was only too aware of the temptations and traps offered by that environment. The fact that Philips, like the inspector, had risen above it, obtained an education, and made it to Mars said more than the possibility that some youthful indiscretions lurked in his past.

Philips was a small man, only a few centimeters taller than Ortiz, slight of build yet with that wiry hint of strength that seemed so common amongst long term residents of Mars. Though only in his early thirties, his sandy hair was already thinning. His face was pinched and taut and in no way could be considered handsome. McKernan decided that Philips would have to be handled gently if they were to get anything out of him.

"Thank you for coming," McKernan said. "I have a few questions for you. We're just trying to pin down where everybody was and what they were doing the night that Dr. Augustyn was killed. Could you tell us what you did that evening?"

"I had dinner, went to my room, and then went to bed," Philips said sullenly.

"And what time was that?"

"I don't know. Probably about 22:00. I wanted to get up early the next morning. Dr. MacKensie had told me that the storm was dying off and the scientists might be able to get out the next morning. They always have a bunch of last minute things they want taken care of, so I wanted to get up and have time to finish breakfast before they started asking for things."

"So you went to your room right after dinner?"

"I helped Molly clear the tables and clean up a bit. I went to my room right after that. About 20:00, 20:30."

"And in the morning, what did you do?"

"I got up at 06:30. Took a shower and went and had breakfast. I was just clearing my tray when Dr. MacKensie came into the dining room to tell us that Dr. Augustyn was dead."

"So you didn't go into the lab that morning?"

"No. Not until after Dr. MacKensie came out. And then he wanted me to put a lock on the door and turn off the heat so the body wouldn't be disturbed before you got here."

"And you did that right away?"

"Yes."

"And to the best of your knowledge no one else entered Dr. Augustyn's office?"

"Well, Molly was there. She looked into the office to make sure Dr. Augustyn was dead, but I don't think she went in. I wasn't there for a couple of minutes while I went to get tools and a lock and hasp. Dr. MacKensie kept all the others out until I had locked it up. Then I gave him the keys."

"Ok. After you went to bed, did you hear any of the others come in?" McKernan asked.

"Sure. Dr. Morand came in not too long after I did. I heard Dr. MacKensie come in around midnight. Dr. Chen and Dr. Berlanescu came in around 02:15. They were kind of noisy and Dr. Morand told them to be quiet. I think Dr. Frederichson and Dr. Moran had come in a few minutes earlier, but I didn't hear them. I never heard Dr. Jensen come in, and I didn't see him in the morning."

McKernan didn't think it was necessary to mention that Dr. Jensen had spent the night elsewhere.

"You know, none of the others seem to remember where you were that night. That's curious, isn't it?"

"No. Why should it be? They never really notice me unless they need me for something."

"Do you have a problem with that?" McKernan asked.

"No. They treat me ok. It's not like they pick on me, or anything. They just don't notice me. I'm part of the station, like the furniture or the power plant."

"But you didn't resent the way they treated you?"

"Mostly they just left me alone, which was ok with me. Not Molly, of course. She was always nice. She kept asking me if I was getting enough to eat. And Dr. MacKensie was always asking me how I was and if I had the right tools and parts and things."

"But the others?"

"Oh, they were all right. Dr. Berlanescu and Dr. Chen would joke around a little, but they didn't mean anything about it. And Dr. Jensen, Dr. Oddsdottir, and Dr. Morand were always polite. But they're scientists. Mostly they are wrapped up in their work. That's ok."

"What about Dr. Augustyn?" McKernan asked.

Philips, whose eyes had been focused on the table top, looked up suddenly.

"How did he treat you?" McKernan repeated.

"He didn't like me," Philips said reluctantly. "He was always on me about paperwork and the way I did my job. But he was like that to Dr. Chen and the others, too." There seemed as if there might be more, but Philips wasn't going to talk about it.

"Let's leave that topic, then," McKernan said. "You are responsible for maintaining things around here. That includes the airlocks and the security system. Is that right?"

"Yeah. Pretty much everything. During the season when the place is full of scientists, they might bring in a few more people to help out, but at a quiet time like this, it's just me unless something major like the reactor goes wrong."

"So can you figure out any way that someone could get past the security on the lab airlock?"

"No. The system is pretty simple, so there really isn't any way to hack it that I know of. An alarm sounds when the airlock doors are open. There's a computer to log events at each airlock. It's built into the lock and you can't get at it without tearing the lock apart. That includes a timestamp and a digital image. Events are also recorded by the central computer. The wiring is all buried in the walls. If anyone had got at that I'd know, and I checked."

"Yet, there's no record of anyone entering or leaving the lab between the time Dr. Augustyn went in at 24:13 and Dr. MacKensie entered at 07:02 the next morning. How do you explain that."

"Simple. No one went through the airlock. If they had, it would have been logged."

"How did someone get into the lab then to kill Dr. Augustyn?" McKernan persisted.

"I don't know," Philips shrugged. "That's your job, isn't it?"

"Are there any other ways into the lab?"

"Just the main lock at the far end of the building. But it's logged as well."

"And nothing shows up, does it?" McKernan asked again.

"No. I checked that morning, both at the central computer and at the logs themselves."

"Why did you do that?"

"I figured that someone would be asking sooner or later. Besides, I didn't like the idea of someone running around killing people."

"Understandable," McKernan said. Despite the fact that Philips wasn't being very cooperative, McKernan got the sense he wasn't lying either.

"We found that access panel on the outside yesterday. Are there any other entry points we don't know about?"

"No. Well, there are some panels that can be removed, but they would breach the envelope and cause a loss of pressure. That would trigger all sorts of alarms. There are probably a dozen pressure sensors in the lab rigged to go off if the pressure or mix gets below set limits. Most of them are sealed units with internal backup power so that they work even if there's a power failure. Just about every building on Mars has those."

McKernan knew that Philips was right about that. Martians tended to be paranoid about loss of pressure, whether it was in a suit, a buggy, or a building. He knew that is own place in Hut Town had three of them.

"So you're saying that the only person to enter the lab wing between the time Dr. MacKensie left at midnight and when he reentered in the morning was Dr. Augustyn? And no one else was in the lab during that time?"

"That's what the logs say. And I'm pretty sure everyone was at dinner. And after dinner Dr. Chen and the others were playing cards. They could see the lab airlock. They could see all three, for that matter. And they were up playing cards until 02:00. Why don't you ask them?"

"I have," McKernan said. "And they all agree that no one used the airlock except for Dr. MacKensie and Dr. Augustyn. Seems impossible, doesn't it?"

"Yeah," Philips concurred. "It's got me stumped."

"How'd you end up on Mars, anyhow, Philips?" McKernan asked, changing the subject.

"I was always good fixing things a kid. I got a company scholarship to tech school from United Semiconductor when I was eighteen. Of course it meant that I had to work for the company for five years after I graduated to pay off the cost of schooling, but, hey, that was all right with me. It meant I had a real job, and you know what that's worth?"

McKernan did, all right. He had chosen the military for much the same reason. That was why there were a hundred applicants for every the company scholarship. An education and practically a guaranteed job was not something one ignored. Not if you grew up in the slums of Earth.

"So you worked for United Semi?"

"Yeah. I did a couple of years on Earth, then they sent me to the Moon for a couple of more. It wasn't bad, and the pay was good. I did ok. They offered me a job on Mars if I'd sign a five year contract extension. The money was even better, and I thought Mars would be better than the Moon any day, so I signed up."

From what McKernan knew of the mining operations on the Moon, Mars was better. A lot better.

"Anyway, I was working for United Semi at one of the mining camps doing maintenance. Suits, buggies, life support, that kind of thing. Then the company got in trouble with the U.N. I didn't have anything to do with that. I didn't even know that it was going on. It was all on the other side of the planet. But you'd know more about that than me."

McKernan did know. He was the man responsible for United Semi losing their mining concession over the Morrison affair.

"Anyway, there I was, out of a job and about to be shipped back to Earth with all the other honest employees of United Semi. That's when Dr. MacKensie offered me a job at Station Alpha. I don't know how he found out about me, but he tracked me down while I was waiting for a ship back to Mars. There were so many United Semi people going home that some of us were stuck in Mars City for months with no pay. I jumped at the chance."

"You didn't want to go back to Earth?" McKernan asked.

"Would you? I figured I'd be just another technician that had been let go by one of the companies. Besides, Mars ain't a bad place. You get used to it. It don't pay as much as United Semi, but I'm pretty much my own boss."

"So you like it here at Station Alpha?" McKernan asked.

"Sure. Molly is nice to me and Dr. MacKensie has always treated me right. I get to fix things, and mostly the scientists are ok to work with."

Time had dragged on, and McKernan had one more interview to conduct.

"I think that will be all the questions for the moment. Thank you for your cooperation," McKernan said.

"I can go?" Philips asked uncertainly.

"Yes."

After he had left, McKernan looked at Ortiz. "Well, what do you think?"

"I'd say he's our prime suspect. If anyone could hack the lock alarms it would be Philips."

"But you just don't see it, do you?"

"No. I guess I don't," Ortiz agreed.

"So that still leaves us with a locked building that no one entered or left during the time the murder was committed and no real suspects. Let's hope that Dr. MacKensie can tell us something useful."

Interview –
Dr. William MacKensie
Day 4, 10:30-11:00

As Dr. MacKensie came into the conference room and sat down, McKernan said," I know that we've gone over this before, but this is for the record. I'm sure you understand?"

"Of course, Inspector. I've spent a lifetime working for various institutions and on different grants. Trust me, I know the dictates of bureaucracy only too well," the station head said affably.

"Well, to start with, why don't you tell me what you did the night before Dr. Augustyn was killed?"

"I had dinner, as usual. I went to my office at around 20:00 after talking briefly to some of the staff. I worked for a few hours. Mostly reports and grant proposals. I don't get much opportunity to do real science these days. I left around 24:00. I said a few words to the boys playing cards. I think I mentioned that it was getting late and it looked like we might get a break in the weather the next day. Then I went directly to bed."

"And there was no one else in the lab building while you were there?"

"Not to my knowledge, no. I don't see how there could have been. Everyone had been at dinner, and my office is right next to the airlock between the lab and administration. I had left my door open. I don't like it closed and the walls are so thin it doesn't make much difference in any case. If the alarm had sounded I'm sure I would have noticed."

"Did you see Dr. Augustyn that night?"

"You mean after dinner? No, I must have just missed him from what I've heard."

"And in the morning?" McKernan asked.

"Well, I got up, must have been 06:45 or so, washed, dressed, and then I headed to the lab. I grabbed a cup of coffee, Molly always brews a pot first thing and leaves it on the counter so people can get a cup as they head into the lab. I went to my office to see if there were any e-mails or things I needed to deal with and to check the weather reports, of course. I wanted to see if it would be safe to let people take the buggies out."

"The log says that was at 07:02," McKernan commented.

"That sounds about right."

"The logs also show that it wasn't until 7:39 that you went back to the administration building to announce that Dr. Augustyn was dead. How do you account for that time."

"Well, as I said, I was checking the weather and things. I didn't think James was in his office. He wasn't an early riser as a rule. It gives one the shudders to think that he was sitting there with the hammer in his head all that time. Anyway, after I had checked things I was headed back to Admin to get breakfast. I popped my head in just on the off chance James was there, and of course then I saw him. It was obvious that he was dead."

"One thing has puzzled me, Dr. MacKensie," McKernan said. "If Dr. Augustyn was not an early riser, why did you check to see if he was in his office? And why didn't anyone think it was strange that he went to his office at midnight and was still there two hours later?"

"The truth is, James kept irregular hours. A lot of what he did, both for station administration, and for his own work involved contacting people on Earth. Between the differences in the length of day between the two planets and the various time zones on Earth, that could lead to some strange hours. Add in the delays in communications where it might take a half hour or so to get a reply to a question, well, you understand. It wasn't that unusual for James to spend some late hours in his office. And of course, we didn't know until later that he'd been in there all night."

"Yes, I see," McKernan said. "And after you found the body, what did you do?"

"I shut the door. I've read enough detective stories to know not to touch anything. I went into the dining room and announced that James was dead. I then told Jason to put a lock on the door and asked Molly, she's our medical person, to confirm that he was dead before the door was sealed. Of course she did."

"And no one else was in the lab at that time?"

"No. I told everyone to remain in the dining room until the door was locked."

"Was everyone present at that time?"

"I really can't say. My mind was on other things, as you can imagine. However, I do remember Sigrid, Nils, and Breaker were there. So was David and Tony and I think Sarah and Boris as well. And of course Molly and Jason, who went back into the lab with me. I can't say if Dieter or Sean were there or not. Sorry."

"That's ok. I can't expect that you would pay attention to minor details at a time like that. During the night, did you hear anyone moving around."

"I did hear David and Tony come in rather late. They were a bit noisy. Breaker told them to keep it down. Other than that, no. I'm sure I was the first one up, except maybe for Jason. I think I heard him moving around as I got up."

"I know this next question is difficult, Dr. MacKensie, but do you have any idea who killed Dr. Augustyn?"

The station head looked thoughtful for a moment. "No, I'm afraid not. I just can't envision any one of them as a murderer."

"As we've interviewed the others, it's become evident that many, if not most of them had some reason to hold a grudge against Dr. Augustyn."

"Yes, well, James was not a nice man. Frankly, I think he was a bit of a sociopath. I was against him being here this season, but you know how it is with funding organizations. And money talks. His being here came with quiet a hefty grant. Also, I think that there was a feeling on the part of some of our supporters that Station Alpha was becoming too much of a one man show. Let's face it. I'm getting on in years and there are concerns about who would replace me if that should be necessary. Not that James would have been interested, of course. Too far from the limelight and fleshpots of Earth, you understand. But I think he may have been expected to make a report on how things were going when he got back to Earth."

"And how did you feel about that?"

"Well, to some extent I do understand the concerns. I've been talking it over with some of the other old hands in Mars science. People like Sigrid and Nils for instance. About spreading the responsibility around a bit. That's part of the reason that I asked them here for this session."

"The other part being?" McKernan asked.

"Oh, to impart their experience to the youngsters, of course. All of the youngsters this season are up and coming in their fields, but I wanted to give them a chance to work with and learn from the people that had been here before them. And I have to say that Breaker, Nils and Sigrid have been doing an admirable job at that."

"Getting back to Dr. Augustyn—" McKernan said.

"Yes. Well, if you've talked to the others I'm sure you know about Nils' marriage and Breaker's research. But that all happened in the past and I'm quite sure they've put it behind them. And I know that James made unwanted advances, perhaps with threats, towards Sigrid and Dr. Toranaga, but I'm don't think they paid any attention to them. Certainly Sigrid can handle herself. You don't, as a woman, get to be as successful in academe without learning how to deal with, shall we say, male chauvinism, to use a term from another age."

"Well what about Dr. Federenkov, Dr. Chen, and the others. I understand Dr. Augustyn had made threats against their careers."

"The reality, for all his political clout, James had a tendency to overestimate his power in such matters. Over the years he'd rubbed enough people the wrong way that the people that really matter tended to ignore him in such things. Besides, they're all the best of the best of the upcoming crop."

"But might one of them feel threatened?"

"Oh, I don't think so. I've had a talk with each of them in private to put their minds at ease."

"You take a proprietary interest in the people here, don't you?" McKernan remarked.

"Of course. Mars has become my life, and these people are, in a way, my legacy."

"What about Jason Philips. He's certainly not in the mold of the others?"

"No," MacKensie agreed, "but he is very good at what he does. And I've learned long ago that world needs more than generals. Besides, his story is unfortunate. I know you know far more than I do about the situation with United Semiconductor, but most of their people had no idea what was going on. Yet they were the ones that were going to have to pay the price. A friend of mine, one of the geologists at United Semi, mentioned Jason's case to me, and said that I couldn't ask for a better man if I was looking for someone with his talents. I looked into it and agreed, so

I offered him a job. It really was a case of being in the right place at the right time."

"But I get the feeling that Dr. Augustyn might have held something over him. Something he was blackmailing him with. You wouldn't know anything about that?"

"No, I can't say that I do," Dr. MacKensie said. "But then, how many of us have an unblemished past. Still, Jason has worked for me for almost three years. I can't see him being violent. It just isn't in his nature."

"He would seem to be the most likely suspect, though," McKernan said. "If anyone could get past the alarms on the airlocks, it would be the person responsible for maintaining them."

"But there's no evidence that they have been tampered with, though. Is there?"

"No, there isn't," McKernan said. "But it's obvious that Dr. Augustyn didn't bury that hammer in the back of his own head, isn't it?"

"It is a puzzler," the station head said. "But I'm sure you'll work it out in the end."

"I wish I was as sure, Dr. MacKensie," McKernan replied.

After Dr. MacKensie left McKernan leaned back and pushed his chair away from the table.

"Well, what do you think?"

Ortiz laughed. "After what I've heard the last two days, I think I would have killed him myself. What a bastard."

"OK. Where were you the night of the murder?" McKernan responded.

There was a moment of silence, then Ortiz said, "You're serious, aren't you?

"Not really, but we might as well put it on record."

"I was doing my normal patrol of the road the day before. I spent the night at Junction 4, before coming back the next day. I was there when I got the report of Augustyn's death. I have witnesses."

"Good," McKernan said with a smile. "I didn't think it was you, but by your own admission, you have about as good a motive and as little opportunity as any of the real suspects. Let's face it, we've got twelve people, eleven of whom have some reason to hate Augustyn's guts, and twelve people who have pretty solid alibis, and that's not counting the fact that no one could have entered or left the lab wing between the time Augustyn entered and the time that MacKensie found the body, at least according to the airlock log."

"So what do we do now?" Ortiz asked.

"Good question. I'm not sure. In mystery novels this is where the detective makes a list of all the suspects and the points for and against.   After that, they usually sit and scratch their heads."

"Do you have a better idea?" Ortiz asked.

"Not really, unless you noticed something I didn't."

"Well, then, why don't we go over all the suspects and summarize the interviews. For the record, as you said."

McKernan smiled. Ortiz was starting to loosen up a bit. "OK. Is the recorder on?"

"It is now," Ortiz said as she punched a button.

"One, Sigrid Oddsdottir. She had been harassed and her career threatened by the victim early in her career while a post-doc. She thinks Augustyn was a sexist pig and a bad scientist. She says that she spent the night with Nils Jensen which he confirms. Two other witnesses, Toranaga and MacDougal say she never left the women's wing all night."

"Two, Sarah Toranaga. She was being harassed by Augustyn and her boy friend Boris Federenkov was being threatened as well. Oddsdottir and MacDougal vouch that she didn't leave the women's wing."

"Three, Molly MacDougal. Her husband died on a flight to pick up the victim, a flight that should never have happened except Augustyn insisted.   Toranaga and Oddsdottir both vouch for her being in the women's wing all night. At least they heard her snoring."

"Four, Nils Jensen. The victim had an affair with his wife that led to their divorce. Oddsdottir says that he spent the night in her room from around 22:00 till 07:30. There is no evidence that he left her room during the night."

"Five, Roger Morand. The victim stole his research and might have ruined his career if MacKensie hadn't intervened. Federenkov places him in the men's wing at 21:30. Told David Chen to keep it quiet at 02:15."

"Six, Boris Federenkov. Augustyn was threatening his career because he wanted to move in on Toranaga.

Federenkov didn't seem too worried. Was seen entering the men's wing at 19:00. Talked to Morand at 21:30. Heard MacKensie at 24:00."

"Seven, David Chen. Augustyn had been giving him a hard time. Threatening his career. Played cards with Berlanescu, Friederichson, and Moran until 01:50. Entered the men's wing with Berlanescu at 02:12. Morand told him to be quiet at 02:15."

"Eight, Antonio Berlanescu. Augustyn also gave him a hard time. Basically throwing his weight around. Played cards until 1:50, entered the men's wing with Chen at 02:12."

"Nine, Dieter Friederichson. Clashed with Augustyn over a research grant. Played cards until 01:50. Entered the men's wing at 01:55 with Sean Moran."

"Ten, Sean Moran. Clashed with Augustyn over planned research. Played cards until 01:50. Entered the men's wing at 01:55 with Friederichson."

"Eleven. Jason Philips. Augustyn was always riding him. He seemed to have something that he was holding over Philips, something in his past which would have resulted in his being sent back to Earth. Was seen going into the men's wing around 19:00. Dr. MacKensie things he heard him get up around 06:30.

"And finally, Dr. MacKensie. No known motive. Four witnesses saw him leave the lab and enter the men's wing at 24:00. Two people, Philips and Federenkov talked with him shortly thereafter. Recorded leaving the men's wing around 07:00 the next morning."

"To summarize the time line according to the airlock logs:

Before 24:00everyone except for Chen, Berlanescu, Frederichson, Moran, and MacKensie are in either the men's or women's wing

24:00	Dr. MacKensie leaves the lab
24:12	Dr. Augustyn enters the lab
02:00	Frederichson and Moran enter the men's wing
02:11	Chen and Berlanescu enter the men's wing
06:15	Molly leaves the women's wing
07:00	Dr. MacKensie leaves the men's wing
07:02	Dr. MacKensie enters the lab
07:15	Most of the others enter the dining room
07:39	Dr. MacKensie leaves the lab and reports the death

"You can stop the recording," McKernan said. Ortiz pressed another button.

"So, what does that leave us with. Eleven people with various motives for hating the victim's guts. Everybody supports everybody else's alibi. The airlock logs support the alibis, too. They were all snug in their beds at the time of the murder."

"What if they were all in it together?" Ortiz suggested. "Or at least a number of them. The airlock log only records when the door opens and takes a picture at that moment. If a number of them were working together, one of them could have followed Augustyn into the lab at 24:12, killed Augustyn, and then left the lab, somehow avoiding the camera, at the time that we think MacKensie entered the lab in the morning."

"This is Station Alpha, Ortiz, not the Orient Express," McKernan said sarcastically.

"Huh?"

"Murder on the Orient Express. It's a classic mystery by Agatha Christie. Twelve people on a train stuck in the snow, all with a motive to kill a thirteenth person. So they all commit the crime and provide alibis for each other. You should read it. But this isn't a mystery novel. For it to be possible would have required that the four card players and Dr. MacKensie were in cahoots at least, and probably Molly. I just don't see that."

"No. I guess you're right. Well, maybe we should examine those motives, sir. Nobody liked Dr. Augustyn, but I don't think they all had a motive to kill him."

"Go on. I'd like to hear what you have to say," McKernan encouraged.

"Well, some of these things happened a long time ago. I think people have moved on. For example, Dr. Oddsdottir, it was years ago that Augustyn harassed her. If he tried it today, she'd just laugh in his face. And Dr. Morand, maybe Augustyn did steal his research, but he's a big man in his field now and I don't think he really cares anymore. Dr. Jensen didn't seem all that upset that his marriage failed."

"As for the four card players, they may have felt that Augustyn was a petty tyrant and an annoying bureaucrat, but in the end, he really couldn't do anything to them. Anytime it really mattered, Dr. MacKensie intervened."

"Toranaga just thought of him as a dirty old man and Federenkov is too wrapped up in his work and Toranaga to really care. They're both on track for tenure. Augustyn really couldn't touch them despite his threats."

"So that leaves Molly MacDougal and Philips," McKernan commented.

"I just don't see Molly killing anyone, at least in that cold blooded way. I talked to her a little last night. She doesn't seem to be the kind of person who lives in the past. She just seems to be at peace with herself. But you know her better than I do."

"I knew her husband a lot better than I know her, but I hope you're right. What about Philips."

"Philips certainly has a motive. He's also responsible for the stations maintenance. If anyone could figure out a way around the airlock logs or some other way of getting into the lab without being detected, he'd be the one."

"Yeah, I think you're right. I think we'll need to poke around a bit.   Maybe there's a secret passage or something."

"Who's been reading too many mysteries, now?" Ortiz joked.

"You know, sir, there is one more person you didn't mention just now, Dr. MacKensie."

"Well he doesn't have a motive as far as I know. And at least five people put him in the men's wing between 24:00 and 07:00."

"There's got to be something we're missing, sir."

"Yes, but what? Let's go to lunch."

CHAPTER 14
DAY 4, 11:30-13:00

Lunch was a quiet affair of toasted ham and cheese on rye sandwiches and a vegetable soup. After the analysis of the interviews both McKernan and Ortiz had come to the realization that they weren't any farther along in solving the mystery of Augustyn's death than when they had arrived at Station Alpha two days earlier. They were still faced with the fact that everyone seemed to have a solid alibi and no one had the opportunity to enter the lab building undetected to commit the murder.

"So what do we do now?" Ortiz asked after she had sopped up the last of the soup with a piece of bread.

"Frankly, I don't know. I've run out of ideas. We've looked at all the physical evidence, the computer logs, Augustyn's files. Everyone has got a motive and everyone's got half a dozen people as an alibi. I'm at the point where I'm thinking of wrapping it up here and heading back to Mars City tomorrow. I hate to give up, but I don't feel like wasting any more time here."

"So what happens if we don't find the murderer?"

"Your guess is as good as mine. I'll file a report, the governor will send it on to some commission on Earth, they'll make a decision based on politics, which probably means they'll do nothing. But the fact remains that Augustyn is dead and everyone knows that one of a dozen people did it. There's not enough grounds to act against any of them, but it won't do any of their careers any good to have the suspicion hanging over them."

Ortiz just grunted in response. She had enough experience as a policewoman to know that not all cases get solved.

"If we're planning on heading back tomorrow, I should make sure the buggy is fueled up and ready to return," Ortiz said finally, getting up.

"Yeah, why don't you do that. I think I'll sit here and decide what I'm going to tell Garcia-Gomez."

As Ortiz went through the lock to the lab building the alarm sounded briefly as if to taunt McKernan. He stared at what was left in his coffee cup. Something was nagging at him, like there was one more thing to look at. But try as he might, he couldn't pin it down. Finally, he picked up his tray and took it over to the kitchen window.

In all the mystery novels, McKernan thought, this is the point when the detective returns to the scene of the crime where he discovers the overlooked clue that lets him solve the case. If only real life was so neat. But the hell of it was he didn't have any better ideas. He walked over to the airlock between the buildings and went through the hatch.

The padlock was still on the office door. He fished the key out of his pocket and opened it, taking a long look around the tiny room. Other than the fact that the body had been removed, it was just as they had left it after taking the photos and dusting for prints.

There wasn't much to it. A desk, an office chair, another chair to the side of the desk, some adjustable shelves along the walls held up by the typical system of standards and brackets. The desk wasn't much, a plastic fake wood grained top about 150 x 60 centimeters, a set of drawers on one side and a cabinet on the other. Like most Earthside furniture on Mars, it had been made to knock down flat for shipping to take up a minimum of space and weight, and then be reassembled once it reached its destination. The sides had large cutouts to keep the weight down. Even the sides and bottoms of the drawers were full of holes.

The chair wasn't much more substantial, but then with the lower gravity of Mars it didn't have to be. The frame was made out of bent aluminum tubing with a fabric back and seat. McKernan noticed with a bit of distaste that some of Augustyn's blood still clung to the back forming a dried brown stain.

He sat down in the seat facing the desk, seeing what the dead man had seen just before the hammer slammed into his skull. There wasn't much to see, a standard computer screen and keyboard took up the center of the desk. There was an "IN" and an "OUT" basket with a few sheets of paper in each. McKernan looked through them. They all seemed to be requisition forms. He noted wryly that paper was still needed in this day and age. The rest of the desktop was bare except for a notepad and a pen. There were no mementoes, no pictures of friends or family, nothing personal.

It was a sharp contrast to the office of MacKensie across the hall. There the walls were covered with pictures of the station chief and coworkers against various Martian and Terrestrial backdrops, mostly of a geological nature. A big chunk of rock took up one corner of the desk. McKernan didn't know why, but he had no doubt that it had some deep personal meaning for MacKensie. There was none of that here. The office was just a temporary place where Augustyn conducted business.. And a place for him to die.

He knew Augustyn's log on for the computer, but he didn't bother to turn it on. Ortiz had been through all the files both on the local drive and those that Augustyn had cached on the network. It was all just what you'd expect, reports, budgets, expenses. There had been some correspondence with people back on Earth, but it all had been of a professional nature, a lot of it having to do with the new position he was assuming upon his return to Earth.

So what was he missing? He looked around the room. There wasn't much. The shelves on the wall were half bare. A few reference books, some printouts, the odd piece of equipment, a pair of binoculars, a microscope, a geologist's hammer that was the duplicate of the one that had ended up in Augustyn's skull. People coming to Mars tended not to bring much with them because of the expense of transportation. They didn't accumulate much for the same reason. Not if they were planning to return to Earth. It was funny, he thought, how you could tell the real Martians by the way they started to collect things once they made the decision not to go back.

The only thing that seemed out of place was a picture hanging on the wall. It was a Mars view, and McKernan thought that it matched the view out the dining room window. Oddly enough, it wasn't a photo or a digital print. It was a water color. Someone must have painted it sitting in the recreation room. He doubted that it had belonged to Augustyn. It probably had come with the office and Augustyn had had no reason to remove it. He'd have to ask MacKensie about it. Whoever had painted it had been quite good. It wasn't detailed and sharp like a digital print, but somehow it captured the Marsness of the scene.

McKernan was curious now and he got up to examine the picture. There wasn't a signature on the front. Thinking there might be some information written on the back he lifted the picture off its hook and flipped it around. There was a name that he didn't recognize and a date from two years earlier, shortly after the station had opened. There was something else, as well. Stuck into a corner of the frame was a semi-transparent strip of black plastic about 15 cm. long and 2 wide.

McKernan pulled it out from where it had been stuck in the frame. He knew what it was, though most people in a digital age wouldn't, it was a piece of developed photographic film. He held it up to the light. He could see there was something on it. It looked like it might be documents, but the images were too small for him to see. He remembered the microscope on the shelves. He grabbed it and placed it on the desk.

It was a typical binocular microscope, not terribly high powered, made to examine the surface of rock samples. He placed the film on the stage and fiddled with the focus knobs. As the film came into focus, he discovered that it was upside down. He flipped it over and refocused. The natural curvature of the film meant that not all of the film would be in focus at once, but there was enough that he could tell what he was looking at.

It was a series of images of documents, eight in all, arranged on the length of film. What in the world was this, he thought. And was it Augustyn's? He found that by pressing down on the film with his finger he could flatten it out to the point where he could make out most of a document. The first one seemed to be some sort of police report in Russian. His knowledge of the language was sketchy at best, but he could read enough Cyrillic to recognize a name, Boris Federenkov. He also recognized the name of the current internal security apparatus in Russia. They always seemed to go in for that kind of thing.

He looked at the next image. It was another police report, this one from Australia. It seemed Dr. Morand had been arrested for participation in a drunken brawl at the age of 19. Embarrassing, but hardly surprising. The next was an automobile accident report involving Dr. Jensen. Alcohol had been involved, but he had been a passenger, not the driver.

There couldn't be much doubt that the film belonged to Augustyn. It seemed that he had been collecting dirt on his colleagues. But why? Spite? Blackmail? By keeping it on film and not on a computer, he could control access to the information and pull it out, or threaten to pull it out when he felt the need to.

The next image was more interesting. Another arrest report, this one for Jason Philips, age 16 from Los Angeles. This was more serious, it involved possession with intent to sell. Because he was a minor at the time, the records should have been sealed, and if Philips hadn't gotten into any trouble later, should never come to light. But if they did, U.N. policy was clear. He would lose his job and be sent back to Earth. For a small fry like Philips, there wouldn't be any exception.

McKernan had grown up in the same kind of neighborhood that he expected Philips had. There were a few things that had happened back then that wouldn't look to good on his own record. There could be no doubt that if Augustyn was threatening to expose Philips, it gave Philips a motive, a strong motive to kill Augustyn. But if he had killed Augustyn, why hadn't he taken the film?

CHAPTER 15
DAY 4, 13:00-14:30

As he sat there staring at the film in the microscope, his phone beeped with the tone he had programmed for Ortiz.

"McKernan here. What is it, Ortiz?"

"Sir, I'm in the locker room by the airlock. I think there's something you should see."

"Is it important?" he asked, knowing it was a dumb question. Ortiz wouldn't waste his time.

"Yes sir," Ortiz answered without emotion.

"I'm in Augustyn's office. I'll be there in a couple of minutes," he answered, clipping his phone back onto his belt. He removed the film from the microscope, wrapped it in a piece of paper from the desk and put it in his pocket.

It was actually less than a minute before he reached the locker room. Ortiz was holding the environment pack from one of the surface suits. She had the cover off and was poking around at the innards. With surprise, he noted that it was the pack from his own suit.

"What is it?" he asked.

"I was checking over my suit before tomorrow, just to make sure it was ready." Like most Martians, Ortiz was obsessed with keeping personal equipment in working order. McKernan had been planning on checking his own suit later this afternoon. "Everything looked okay, but just to be sure, I ran a pressure check and a diagnostic. That's when I found it."

"Get on with it. What did you find?"

"The environment pack had been sabotaged. The spring that works the mixture valve snapped. Not right away, but after a few minutes. That should never happen. On a hunch I checked your suit, too. The same thing had been done. That's when I called you."

"Same spring?"

"Yes. And whoever did it was real clever. You couldn't tell just by looking. I'm not sure, but it almost looks like they made a substitute spring out of something more brittle. Either that or treated normal springs to have the same effect."

"That would take someone with specialized knowledge, wouldn't it?"

"Yeah. You never know with science types. Some of them are pretty good machinists from building experimental equipment, but I'd be surprised if one of the science crew did this."

"Which means, maybe we should have a talk with Jason Philips. What would have been the results if we had been out on the surface and the spring broke?"

"I don't think it would have been fatal, at least if we were close to a building or a buggy. The emergency backup would still be able to supply five to ten minutes of breathable air. But we'd have had to get inside and repair the suits before we could go anywhere. It might have taken some time to find the problem and fix it. Maybe an hour or two. It's not normally the kind of thing you expect."

"But what was the point? If it wasn't to kill us. A warning? Were we getting too close to someone? Or did whoever do this want to delay us? And if so, from doing what?"

"I don't know, sir," Ortiz answered. "But if I hadn't found it and we were between here and Junction Three tomorrow, it might have caused us some problems."

"Do you think your buggy might have been sabotaged as well?"

"I doubt it. I've kept it on lock down since we got here. I ran diagnostics earlier, before I checked out the suits. I think it should be okay."

"Good. Why don't you track down Philips and bring him here. I want to see what he says when we confront him with the evidence."

"Right, sir," Ortiz said and turned to leave. McKernan noticed that she was undoing the flap on her sidearm as she left.

He checked over his suit. Not that he didn't trust Ortiz. If anything, she was more careful than he was. But you didn't survive six years on Mars without learning to check things twice. He was still poking around the environment pack when she returned five minutes later.

"He isn't in any of the buildings. I checked the logs for the locks and there was an access on the one at the end of the men's wing about fifteen minutes ago. That was right after I called you. I did a quick check on the location of everyone at the station. Chen and Berlesconi are out in one of the buggies doing field work. So are Jensen and Sigridsdottir. I could find everyone else except Philips. I took a quick peek out a window at the parking area. One of the buggies is missing besides the two that are out in the field."

"You think Philips took it?"

"That would be my guess."

"How soon can we get our suits fixed and after him."

"It shouldn't take more than a few minutes to fix the suits if I can find replacement springs. The buggy is fueled and the enviro packs topped up. With luck, less than half an hour."

"Get on it, then. I'll tell MacKensie. What I want to know is where the hell Philips thinks he's going to go?"

It was more like forty-five minutes before they were in the airlock. Ortiz had insisted on checking the replacement springs before installing them in the suits. McKernan hadn't objected.

He didn't object to Ortiz running one last diagnostic check on the buggy before they headed out, either. They didn't know how long they might be out, or where they were headed. The one thing they could be sure of would be that they wouldn't have any back up. Not unless Philips was headed towards Mars City.

In a way, the recent dust stormed helped. It had covered all the old tracks. It only took them a few minutes to pick up the tracks of Philips' buggy as it headed north from the station. Away from Junction Three. Ortiz drove the buggy in that direction, driving parallel to Philips' track.

"How much range do you think he has?" McKernan asked. He had a good knowledge of the capabilities of most of the common hardware used on Mars, but Ortiz had had a lot more practical experience lately, and had dealt with the Station Alpha equipment before.

"It depends on if he's got any auxiliary tanks of hydrogen on board. Normally, the buggies at the station have a range of about twelve hundred kilometers, but with extra tanks that might be extended to close to two thousand. With only one person aboard, the life support is probably good for two weeks. I guess it all depends on if he was planning to skip out all along or if this was a last minute decision."

"Great. Two thousand kilometers is a hell of a lot of Mars to cover. Where does he think he's going? Or is he just driving out into the desert to die?"

"Nowhere, sir," Ortiz said enigmatically

"Nowhere. Is that a joke?"

"No. There's a prospector's colony about nine hundred kilometers north of here. The official name is Erehwon, from some old book, but most of the miners just call it Nowhere. It's a pretty rag tag group, maybe a couple of dozen people. Halfway self-sufficient. They do some prospecting and mining, mostly rare earths and some scavenging. They grow most of their own food, get their water from buried ice. Use solar cells to break the water into oxygen and hydrogen. Every three months or so one or two of them will make a run to the nearest base to exchange what they've found for supplies. It's a pretty marginal sort of existence, but they're pretty much off the grid. Philips might think that he could hide out there. He might. Those prospectors are a pretty independent bunch and Philips is real good at fixing things."

In a way, McKernan wasn't surprised. Almost from the start, Mars had attracted wildcatters, independent prospectors looking for a new frontier. The corporations hadn't tried to discourage them. In a way, it saved them money. Mars was a big place, much too big for even the big mining combines to survey effectively. It made sense to let the independents take all the risks, physical and financial, and then buy out the claims of the successful ones. The unsuccessful ones kept at it until they ran out of money or luck. Mostly it was the latter. The average lifespan of a prospector was only about three years, but the ones who survived were pretty rugged and could make do with the bare minimum of resources. Usually, they were pretty much loners or small groups of two or three working together, but occasionally they'd group together into little enclaves for mutual support.

"So you think that's where he's headed?"

"It's where I'd go, I guess. Anyplace else, Mars City, any of the big corporate camps, he'd know there'd be constables waiting."

"You know where this Nowhere is?"

"Not exactly. I've never been there, myself, but I think I have a good idea of the general area its located in. Within twenty kilometers, or so." She brought up a map of the terrain ahead of them an pointed out a place with her finger.

McKernan studied the map. Philips had almost an hour and a quarter head start on them, and chances were that Ortiz wasn't that much better a driver, not enough to catch up in a hurry. The one thing in their favor was that Philips couldn't be sure they were on their trail. If he was trying to stretch his resources, he might be playing it safe, not driving at the limit and taking the path with the safest terrain. They might be able to make up some time by not playing it safe.

"Let's assume that Nowhere is where he's headed. I'm going to radio Mars City and see if we can get a better idea of where it's located. Also, maybe we can get a reading on where Philips is by tracking his transponder."

"I thought of that, sir," Ortiz said. "I'm pretty sure he's disabled the transponder on his buggy. It's not hard to do. At least I haven't been able to pick it up using the direction finder. But one of the satellites might be able to pick up his heat signature."

"Yeah, good thinking." He got on the radio. This far out, he had to rely on satellites. There were no relay towers close enough to pick up. Mars didn't have a complete set of commsats yet. There was one in geosynchronous orbit over the equator at the longitude of Mars City, but most communications depended on a set of low altitude satellites following polar orbits. That was the only way to reach higher latitudes, but until the network was complete, there were gaps in the net. He had to wait fifteen minutes before one was over the horizon. After that, it didn't take long to get through. Five minutes later, Gaeretts got back to them with the coordinates for Nowhere. He also said that he had requested a scan to try and pinpoint Philips, but it might take a while. He'd get back to them when he had more information.

Half an hour later he came back on the radio.

"They were able to spot both you and Philips from the satellite. He's about forty kilometers ahead of you. I'm haven't been able to spot any short cuts. You may have to chase him all the way to Nowhere. Do you want us to send some men with a plane to wait for him?"

"No. At least not for the moment. If he sees a plane waiting he might just head out into the desert. Is there anyone within driving range?"

"Lucas at Anglo Martian #5 is maybe a day and a half away in the other direction. That's about it in that part of Mars."

"I'll keep that in mind. Tell Lucas to get ready, but to stay put for the time being. Maybe we'll get lucky and catch up to him."

"Good luck, chief."

"Thanks. McKernan out."

"Well you heard. Do we have enough fuel to get to Nowhere?"

"Oh, we can make it to Nowhere, all right," Ortiz responded. "It's getting back, that I'm not sure about. That's pushing the limits for what we've got on board, especially if I keep at this pace. Well be running on fumes by the time we get back. Let's hope those prospectors have some hydrogen they're willing to sell."

"You might as well back off a bit, then. I don't think we're going to catch up with Philips in a stern chase before he gets to Nowhere."

Ortiz dropped their speed to thirty-five kilometers per hour.

CHAPTER 17
DAY 4, 18:00-22:00

They kept driving north. The sun was approaching the western horizon and the shadows of the rock formations around them lengthened, making it hard to see the ground in front of them. Ortiz flipped on the buggy's headlights which only helped a little.

"It's going to be getting dark soon. Are we going to keep on going through the night?"

McKernan thought about it, reminded of another chase he had been part of three years earlier, only that time he had been the pursued, not the hunter. The fact was that they had a pretty good idea of where Philips was headed. They also had the advantage of the overhead surveillance that the satellites could provide, even if only intermittently. Mars was a big place, but not so big that it was likely they would lose track of their quarry.

"There's no point in getting ourselves killed," he said. "As soon as you find a good place we can stop for the night."

Ortiz nodded in approval. McKernan noted that the longer they worked together, the more comfortable the constable became.

They drove for another half hour until the sun had set and pulled up in a flat spot in the lee of a low ridge. It was as good a place as any. On Mars one didn't have to worry about the weather except for the occasional dust storm. The last one had finally died down which was usually a signal for a space of quiet conditions. It would get cold during the night, but the buggy was insulated and equipped with a decent heater.

"What's to eat?" McKernan asked after they had stopped and prepped the buggy for the night.

"The usual selection of M.R.E.'s," Ortiz replied with a laugh. The self heating rations were standard fare for the field on Mars. They weren't that different than those that had been used by the military a century earlier. It was a standard joke that they actually were left over from some early twenty first century conflict. At least it was usually a joke. The reality was that if it was shipped from Earth, transportation costs outweighed any other considerations, and so there was no incentive to skimp on quality.

Ortiz rooted around in a storage locker that served as a bench seat along one side of the buggy's interior.

"We've got something labeled chicken casserole, another 'meat-loaf and potatoes', enchiladas with beans and rice, and 'Hungarian goulash.' The enchiladas aren't bad. It comes with hot sauce that helps to mask the flavor. I always try to keep the buggy stocked with that."

"I'm feeling adventurous. I think I'll try the goulash."

Ortiz pulled out two packs from the locker. "Do you feel like orange, grape or cherry drink?"

"You choose. I'm not picky."

Ortiz pulled out a pouch and poured the powder it contained into a liter plastic bottle, adding water from a tap in the wall. She shook the contents vigorously until the bottle took on a purplish hue. She placed the meal packs and the bottle on a table that unfolded from the floor between the two benches. Another compartment in the wall yielded some cups, plates and tableware. Martians didn't tend to use disposable utensils because of the transportation costs. So far no one was producing anything locally.

They each pulled the heating tabs on their respective meals and filled their cups with the "grape" drink. They ate in silence. The food wasn't actually that bad. Culinary scientists on Earth had had nearly a century to perfect their art. When they had finished, there was still about half the bottle of drink left.

"Would you like some flavoring in your grape?" Ortiz asked.

McKernan raised an eyebrow. "Sure."

Ortiz produced a metal flask from the compartment that had held the plates and cups, and added about two centimeters of a clear liquid to each of their cups before topping them up with the drink.

McKernan took an experimental drink. It actually wasn't too bad.

"Jenny's husband at Junction 3 makes it from potatoes and anything else he has. He calls it vodka. I'm not going to argue."

"I've had a lot worse."

They drank in silence for a few minutes, then Ortiz asked, "Do you really think Philips did it?"

"I don't know," McKernan replied. He had told Ortiz about the microfilm as they had been driving. "He had a motive, but did he have the opportunity? We still don't know how anyone could have gotten into the lab between the time that Augustyn entered and the time MacKensie found the body."

"Philips could have tampered with the record or the alarm," Ortiz commented.

"Maybe. But if he did, he didn't leave any trace."

"He was the person responsible for maintaining the system."

"I know. If we'd found any evidence of tampering, he'd be the one I'd suspect. But we didn't find it. And the alarm is pretty well tamper proof. We know it was working when Augustyn entered the lab because the card players all claimed to have heard it. And we have a witness that it was working when MacKensie entered in the morning."

"Well, if he didn't do it, why did he tamper with our suits?" Ortiz asked. "And why did he run?"

"That's a good question. Why did he tamper with our suits? He wasn't trying to kill us. At worst it would have delayed us an hour or two. And if he was trying to make a clean getaway, why call attention to himself. It's almost as if he wanted us to follow him out here."

"So you don't think he did it?" Ortiz asked skeptically.

"I don't know. It just doesn't add up. But I'm damned if I've got a better idea. Do you?"

"I'm as puzzled as you are."

"I do know, speaking as a policeman, when someone runs, you go after them. They might not be the culprit, but there's a good chance that they know something, or at least think they do. When we catch Philips I've got some questions for him."

"Well, we should catch up with him tomorrow," Ortiz said. "I figure we should be able to get to Nowhere by sunset tomorrow. If Philips isn't there, then he's just driving into the desert until he runs out of fuel."

"Well, let's clean up and get some sleep so we can get started at first light," McKernan said, picking up the plates and taking them to the tiny area provided for washing up. Ortiz folded the table back into the floor. Two narrow cots popped out of recesses in the walls above the benches.

"Are we going to set watches?"

"I don't see much point. The satellite put him fifty kilo's ahead of us. He's a fool if he doesn't stop for the night. I'd rather that we were both rested and sharp tomorrow when we catch up with him.

The buggy's quarters were pretty cramped, but they managed to get into their cots without bumping into each other.

CHAPTER 18
DAY 5, 06:00-19:00

McKernan woke to the smell of coffee brewing. It was one of the quirks of the supply system on Mars that while coffee was itself a luxury, it was also one of the items included in the freeze dried ration packs the U.N supplied to Trust Authority workers in the field. McKernan had come to associate it with those times he was traveling outside the confines of Mars City.

"It will be light enough to travel in a half hour or so," Ortiz said as she shoved a mug into his hands. He noticed that she had already folded her bunk back into the wall recess where it was stowed while traveling. He got up and did the same with his own before retiring to the little curtained alcove that served as toilet facilities in the cramped interior of the buggy.

When he came back the table had been popped up out of the floor again and two ration packs were waiting on its surface.

"Scrambled eggs and bacon," Ortiz said. She had already pulled the heating tab on her own breakfast.

"How far to reach Nowhere?" McKernan asked, pulling the tab on his own pack.

"A little over five hundred kilometers. We should be able to make it before nightfall. I assume you want to head straight there rather than try to pick up Philips' trail." They had lost the track of the other Mars buggy on some hard ground after the first hundred kilometers the day before.

"That seems to make the most sense unless the satellite sensors show him heading in some other direction," he said, chewing mechanically on a strip of the bacon. He had followed Ortiz's lead and mixed in some hot sauce with the eggs. It helped.

They finished breakfast in silence and cleaned up. Like most Martians, they were both compulsively neat. They were already rolling when the sun peaked up over a low ridge to the east.

As Ortiz drove, McKernan checked the comm. Gaeretts had uploaded the latest infrared shots from the satellite. As he suspected, Philips had stopped for the night as well. He was only a hundred or so kilometers ahead of them and was taking a track just a little off to their right.

"It's going to be a long day. I suggest we take two hour shifts driving."

"That's fine with me. You're the boss." Ortiz's attention was focused on their path, keeping both hands on the controls. The terrain they were driving through wasn't really that bad, practically flat, but there were enough rocks and small craters to avoid that she didn't let herself be distracted except for the occasional sip of coffee.

They switched over driving duties at 08:30. It had been a while since McKernan had driven a buggy on unimproved terrain, but after a half hour or so he fell into the rhythm. Still, he wasn't reluctant to trade back when Ortiz's next stint came.

The view out the buggy's front window was hypnotic. There wasn't much to differentiate one chunk of ground for another. Everything was a monotonous reddish orange hue, and as the sun rose the landscape took on a flat, low relief aspect.

About 11:00 Ortiz gave him a nudge and pointed out the window to their right. It took McKernan a moment to see what she was pointing at, but then made it out, the twin tracks of a Mars buggy, fresh in the fine sand that covered everything. They had picked up Philips' track.

When it came time to switch drivers again, McKernan said, "Let's take a fifteen minute break. We're on Philips' trail, now. I don't think we'll miss him, and I'd rather we were fresh when we do catch up to him."

"Suits me," Ortiz replied. "Do you want some lunch?"

"Good idea," McKernan replied. "What do we have?"

Ortiz got up, stretched her legs, tried to loosen her shoulders in the cramped space of the buggy. There was just enough headroom for her to stand upright. McKernan had to stoop to avoid hitting his head. She did another stretch and then rummaged around in the food locker.

"We've got a bunch of finger food. Tacos and chips, hamburger and chips, or hot dogs and chips. The tacos aren't bad if—"

"Let me guess. They aren't bad if you put hot sauce on them."

"You've got it."

"Tacos are fine with me," McKernan said.

The tortilla on the taco was a bit soggy, but the salsa for the chips had decent flavor. Ortiz mixed some cherry drink without "vodka" to wash it down.

"Mind if I ask you something personal, sir?"

McKernan was a little surprised. So far, Ortiz had gone out of her way to keep things professional on their expedition. "Go ahead," he said, his curiosity aroused.

"You've been on Mars nearly six years. That means your second contract must be about up. Do you think you're going to sign up for a third?"

"Your contract is coming up, too, isn't it?"

"Yeah. I've got nine months left."

"Are you thinking of signing for another stint?"

"I'm thinking about it. That's why I asked."

"Yeah, I'm thinking about it. I don't really have anything on Earth to go back to. No family to speak of. Of course if I stick around another three years it means I'll probably never go back. Nine years is just too much time between. It would be hard to fit in back on Earth, not to mention finding a job that gave me as much freedom and responsibility as I've got here. But if you have any doubts, after the first contract would be the time to go back. Every three years makes it just that much harder."

"Well, I'm thinking of sticking around. I really don't have anyone back on Earth, either. Oh some aunts and cousins, but I was never close, and after four years in the military and three here, not a lot in common. I like what I do. I've also got kind of a boy friend." Ortiz blushed as she said the last. McKernan hadn't thought she could.

"Oh?"

"Yeah. His names Mike. He's the mechanic at Junction Three. He's a nice guy, real handy. He fixes anything that comes in, sells supplies on the side, helps out Jenny and her husband on the farm when they need it. He's working on building a real house next to his shop."

"Sounds like a real find. He doesn't mind you being a cop?"

"No. He understands. And it's not like we face real criminals much."

"Only the occasional murderer. Speaking of which we better get going if we're going to reach Nowhere by sundown."

McKernan took the next shift driving. It was easier now because he could follow the track Philips left.

"You know, I've got a decision to make, too. The guy who owns the hut next to mine is taking a job on the other side of the planet. He's willing to sell his to me at a good price. If I stick around I could fix it up pretty nice. Have a separate bedroom, more room for plants. Even a back door."

"You live in Hut Town?" Ortiz asked in amazement.

"Yeah. It's roomier and quieter than bachelor quarters at the Trust housing. I bought the place I've got now my first year on Mars. It's in one of the more established quieter corridors. Most of my neighbors are pretty good people."

"Sounds nice. Do you have a girl friend?" Ortiz said, then quickly, "Forget I said that."

"No. No romantic entanglements at the moment. Not much time."

"Too bad."

CHAPTER 19
DAY 5, 17:30-19:00

They reached Nowhere with about half an hour of sunlight left. McKernan had been driving, and when they popped over the last ridge between them and the settlement, he halted the buggy at the crest. Ortiz handed him a pair of binoculars and took another pair for herself.

"That's Philips' buggy," he said, pointing at a vehicle that was parked in front of what appeared to be the main building.

Nowhere was a curious contrast. It looked like it was built out of a ramshackle assortment of salvaged materials and repurposed junk, but at the same time it had a look of permanence to it.

The main building looked like one of the early pneumatic huts they had used on the first expedition, maybe ten meters in diameter and thirty long. Above the main lock was a hand painted sign reading "Erewhon."

Attached to the big hut were a string of other huts sticking off tubes that led a hundred meters in either direction from the main building. Some of these huts, particularly the ones in close, were dug in with soil piled over the top to provide some protection from solar radiation. Solar cell panels stuck out anyplace space could be found, a real mixture of models, no two exactly alike. The mountings seemed to be made out of anything that could be found. Off to the side was a big cryotank. It must be for storing hydrogen, McKernan thought, as there was what looked like an electrolysis plant next to it. Water was plentiful on Mars. All you had to do was dig for it, especially as you got closer to the poles. The solar cells could be used to break it down into hydrogen and oxygen. The oxygen could be breathed and the hydrogen used in fuel cells to power buggies and provide electricity. It was less reliable than a reactor, but easier to cobble together. There were also a number of green houses and other auxiliary structures.

Off to one side there was what looked like a parking area. McKernan counted a total of eleven vehicles, though a couple of them looked like they wouldn't run. As far as they could see, no one was running around outside.

"How many people do you think there are?" McKernan asked.

"Hard to say. I've got to think from the number of huts at least twenty men unless they're using them for storage. From rumors I've heard, there are a number of women, too. The green houses look as if they might be able to support three dozen people in a pinch. That's a lot for two cops to take on by themselves."

"Yeah. What have you got for fire power?"

"Not much. No call for it. I've got my side arm, six mm. automatic, three clips of ammo, forty-two rounds in all. I've also got a pump action riot gun, but I'd hate to have to use that inside a building. A load of buckshot could take out a whole wall, with no way to patch it in time to save the air."

"This may be a case when the threat is worth more than the reality. I'd like to think these guys aren't armed with anything more than knives and clubs. There really shouldn't be any unaccounted for firearms on Mars, but I've been proved wrong on that before. After all, this place shouldn't exist, either."

"What are you carrying? Sir," Ortiz asked.

"I've got a 9 mm., a automatic like you stuck in my boot, and a knife in the other one." He got up and reached into his bag. "I've also got this," he said pulling out a long barreled .44 magnum revolver.

"Jesus, that's a cannon. Are you planning to blow in the airlock door?"

"Like I said, intimidation potential may be everything. Are you ready?"

"As ready as I'm going to be."

McKernan drove them down and parked right in front of the airlock door. He stopped the buggy so that it was between the lock and Philips' own buggy. They were already suited up, so it only took a minute until they were out on the surface.

There didn't appear to be any lock on the airlock hatch. It swung open when McKernan operated the controls. Technically, it was a one man lock, but by squeezing, they both managed to fit in the cramped space. McKernan closed the outer hatch and pressed the button to cycle the lock.

While the lock cycled they were vulnerable. The inner hatch was a half inch steel, but a big enough gun could pierce that.   There was an alarm sounding, so there wouldn't be any element of surprise.

The lock finished cycling. McKernan asked, "Ready."

He could see Ortiz nod behind the faceplate of her helmet. He worked the release on the hatch and swung it open. He stepped out, his hand resting on the butt of the revolver. Ortiz, cradling the riot gun in her arms took up a position behind and to his side.

They were in a large room. There were fifteen men standing in a group looking like they arguing about something. They had the lean hungry look typical of prospectors. Most of them looked to be in their late thirties or forties. A couple of women could be seen off in the corner of the room. Surprisingly, there were also a couple of kids, one of whom started crying.

It looked like they hadn't been expected. None of the men seemed to be armed, though a couple had work knifes attached to their belts.

One of the men, grey haired and with a neatly trimmed beard stepped forward. "Who are you?"

"I'm Chief Inspector McKernan, and this is Constable Ortiz. We're in pursuit of a fugitive, the man that came in the Mars buggy outside."

"We don't want no trouble, mister, but how do I know you are who you say?"

"Here are my credentials," McKernan said, and tossed his badge over to the man. He looked at them closely.

"You're the one who got those that killed Morrison, aren't you?" he asked, handing the badge back.

"Yeah. That was me."

"Morrison was a friend of mine. We won't give you no trouble. You've come a long way. Why do you want this guy?"

"He's wanted for questioning in a murder case. A man was killed at Station Alpha."

"Did he do it?"

"I don't know for sure, but he ran. We came after, and I intend to bring him back."

"Well, he's here. He's not one of us. Like I told you, we don't want any trouble with the law. Jake, bring him out here."

A big, burly man stepped from the back of the crowd holding Philips by the arms. Philips had the helmet off of his surface suit. He didn't look like he had been beaten, but it appeared his reception hadn't been that welcoming either.

"I think we can relax, Ortiz," McKernan said, as he popped the seal on his helmet. Ortiz relaxed a little, but still held the shotgun at the ready.

McKernan took off his helmet. It was always easier to negotiate face to face rather than through a helmet.

Philips looked like the fight had gone out of him. "I won't make any trouble, Inspector. I want to confess. I killed Professor Augustyn. I'll go back with you."

CHAPTER 20
DAY 5, 19:00-22:00

"Jason Philips, I arrest you on suspicion for the murder of James Augustyn." Even as he said them, the words sounded strange to McKernan, like some holdover from another time and place. "Ortiz, cuff him."

The constable went about the job with quiet efficiency. Philips made no attempt to resist. McKernan turned back to the man who appeared to be the leader.

"We've had a long drive. I'd like to spend the night if you don't mind. We can supply our own provisions if that's a problem."

"We'd be happy to have you, Inspector. We don't get much company out here. By the way, I'm John Hammond, more or less the mayor of this place." He offered his hand, and McKernan, holstering his pistol shook it.

"Is there some place secure that I can put my prisoner until morning?"

"There's a store room in back. There's no lock, but it's got a strong door with a latch that can't be worked from inside. We can put a pad on the floor so he has someplace to sleep."

"That sounds like it will do fine," McKernan said.

"Jake, show the constable the store room," Hammond said. Ortiz followed the big man who had held Philips towards the rear of the hut.

"I'd offer you dinner, but I'm afraid that we've already finished our evening meal."

"That's ok. I apologize for the lateness of our call." Looking about him, McKernan figured that the settlement was on fairly short rations. None of the people in view looked like they had seen many extra calories in a while. "We've got our own food in the buggy. I would appreciate it though, if there was someplace we could spend the night and a change out of our suits. We've been in them for a day and a half."

"There's an empty room in the hut next door if you don't mind sharing it with your constable."

McKernan smiled. "That will do fine. Anything will be better than another night in the buggy."

When Ortiz returned from locking up Philips, McKernan sent her out to the buggy for some ration packs. While he waited for her return, Hammond led him into a room that seemed to serve as the communal dining room. There were a number of long tables and benches that seemed to have been cobbled together from odds and ends of packing crates and plumbing. Everything about the place had the same patched together look to it, but McKernan noted that it was also tidy and ordered. Hammond showed him a place at the end of one of the tables and then sat across from him as if he was eager for conversation. McKernan noted that most of the settlement seemed to be quietly filing in and finding places at the other tables, motivated by curiosity more than anything.

"You seem to be doing alright for yourselves here," McKernan said.

"Well it ain't easy, but we get by. We manage to grow most of our own food. Water's no problem. There's plenty of ice below the surface if you know where to look, and of course we recycle all we can. We do a bit of prospecting and such to pay for what we can't make or grow ourselves. Some of the men take temporary jobs with some of the mining companies when they need some extra hands to make a little money."

"Still, this is a pretty big settlement," McKernan commented.

"Well we do a lot of salvage, too, when we can," Hammond said, looking to see how McKernan would react.

"Salvage?"

"You needn't look at me like that, Inspector. We don't take anything that belongs to anyone. But you'd be surprised at how much stuff is just left lying around for the picking. If something breaks or wears out, it just gets tossed out in the sand. And it doesn't pay to send anything back to Earth. Costs too much and Earth's got too much of its own junk, anyway. We just pick up the odds and ends that get thrown out or left behind, fix 'em up and sell 'em if we can, figure out a different way to use it if we can't. Lot of prospectors are more than willing to buy stuff from us if it's half the cost of something from Earth. Some of the smaller mining companies, too, for that matter."

McKernan was saved from having to say something by Ortiz's return. She dropped a couple of ration packs on the table and took a seat next to McKernan.

"I gave Philips a bottle of water and a ration pack. Green bean casserole, not one of my favorites. We got pot roast and chicken and rice here. I'll take the chicken unless you object."

"No, pot roast is fine," McKernan said.

"I'm sorry we weren't able to offer you supper, Inspector, but I can offer you something to wet your whistle," Hammond said. "Helen, could you bring over three mugs of the dark?"

"Sure thing, John," a thin, blond woman in her mid forties called from a corner of the room. A moment later she came over carrying three good sized tankards that looked like they had been made from lengths of aluminum pipe with a base welded on.

"Take a sip," Hammond said, grinning.

McKernan did and grinned back. It was beer, dark and slightly sweet. It reminded him of something he'd had in Germany once, while he'd been in the service.

"Where'd you get this?"

"Brewed it ourselves, or at least Helen did. Got the barley from a farmer in trade for some heaters we rigged up for his green houses. Had to grow the hops ourselves."

"I know a friend in Mars City who'd pay good money for this."

"Well, we can only brew enough for our own consumption just now, but if we can get a steady supply of barley, we might consider it. Anyhow, it makes the nights bearable. I'll leave you two to your dinners now."

"Thanks for the beer," McKernan said.

While they were eating their meals, Ortiz said, "I checked our fuel level. We don't have enough to make it back to Station Alpha without topping off the hydrogen, but I checked Philips' buggy. If I take all he has left, we should be able to make it with a good margin for safety. We'd have to leave the station's buggy here, though."

"Well, I'd just as soon we all traveled back in the same buggy, anyway," McKernan said. "I don't think Philips will cause any trouble, but I'd rather play it safe. If the Station wants their buggy back, they can send someone up here to retrieve it, or pay Hammond to drive it back for them. If not, I'm sure it won't go to waste."

"That's what I figured you'd say, so I transferred the fuel already," Ortiz said, sipping her beer. She had been leery of the brew at first, but had warmed up to it.

"So what do you think of the set up here?" she asked.

"It's pretty marginal, at best. One bad break could wipe them out. But it's their choice, and they seem to be making a go of it so far. I guess there will always be some people who just want to get away from where other people tell them what to do."

"Hasn't that always been what drives pioneers?"

"Yeah, the problem is when civilization catches up with them, which it always does. Well that's a problem for the future and hopefully someone else's worry. We've got a long drive ahead of us and I'd like to get going at first light if not earlier."

CHAPTER 21
DAY 6, 05:30-12:30

McKernan wanted to get an early start the next morning. It would be a long drive back to Station Alpha, and he'd prefer it if he didn't have to spend a night out on the surface with a prisoner. Fortunately they had their own outbound track to follow, so they would be able to make better time on the way back. A few of the locals were up and stirring, but they all stayed out of the way, which suited McKernan fine.

When they released Philips from the storage room it he had the look of a man resigned to his fate. While spending the night shackled hadn't done him any physical harm, mentally he had all but shut down.

His movements as he donned his surface suit under the watchful eyes of Ortiz were mechanical. McKernan had to perform the suit checks himself once Philips had twisted his helmet into the docking ring. That just wasn't normal behavior for a Martian. You always checked everything yourself. People who didn't, died. It was as if Philips didn't care whether he lived or died anymore, Which was dangerous, not just for him, but anyone around him. That was all the more reason to get back to Station Alpha as soon as possible.

"OK, Philips. We're going out now. We're taking our buggy and leaving the other one here. Do you understand?"

He gave a barely perceptible nod inside his helmet.

"I'm going out through the lock first." There wasn't room for all three of them in the lock at once. Even two people would be a tight fit. Ortiz was smaller than McKernan, so she got to share the lock with the prisoner.

McKernan entered the lock and cycled through. Once outside he backed up a couple of meters from the outer hatch. He didn't draw his gun, but his hand was on the grip.

The airlock on the hut wasn't the fastest, and it seemed to take forever before the indicator light changed and the hatch opened, though it had probably been all of ninety seconds. Philips stepped out a few paces and stopped, staring ahead blankly.

McKernan pointed at their buggy, though it was hard to miss. It was the closest and the only one with a star painted on the side.

The buggy lock presented another problem. It was strictly a one person affair. Philips would have to cycle through on his own.

"I'll go through first," McKernan said. "Philips, you enter when Ortiz tells you to. Don't worry about the controls. I'll handle that from inside. Do you understand?"

Again, there was a barely perceptible nod.

"Do you understand? Let me hear you say it?" McKernan wanted to make sure he was getting through to him.

"Yes. I understand."

"Good."

McKernan opened the hatch and stepped into the lock. There was barely room to stand up in it, and no room to move around. It took sixty seconds to cycle, then the inner hatch was free. He stepped through into the interior of the buggy, turned around to face the lock hatch. He didn't bother to crack his helmet. He could do that once Philips was secured.

He watched the indicator to see when the outer hatch had opened and closed behind Philips. There was a small window in the hatch, maybe six centimeters in diameter. From where he stood he couldn't see much, but he could tell there was a body in the lock. He pressed the controls to cycle through.

When the indicator showed green he opened the hatch and motioned Philips to sit on the bench that ran along the far side of the buggy while they waited for Ortiz to cycle through. The constable opened the hatch warily. McKernan noted that her hand was resting on the butt of her pistol just as his own was.

The patrol buggy was pretty much a standard issue vehicle. There had been no major modifications for police use. There certainly weren't any special facilities for holding prisoners. There were a variety of restraints stowed in a locker with the hope that there would be something for a variety of levels of compliance.

"OK, Philips. I want you to take your helmet off and hand it to Ortiz. Do it slow and steady."

The prisoner complied.

"OK. Now we've got a long ride in front of us. I can make it relatively comfortable for you or not. It's your choice. If you tell me you won't make any trouble, I'll take you at your word, and we'll just shackle one hand to a ring in the back. You'll be able to sit on the bench and move about a little. But if you give us trouble, we'll have no choice but to shackle your legs and hands and lay you on your back. Do you understand?"

Philips nodded and then said, "I understand. I won't make any trouble."

"Good. Ortiz get the cuff."

She got a handcuff attached to a half meter of chain. One end she fastened to a ring that had been welded to the rear bulkhead. The other end went on Philips's left wrist. It might not be that comfortable, but he'd be able to sit in a jump seat that folded out of the bulkhead and he'd be able to brace himself against the inevitable jostling of the buggy.

Only when the prisoner was settled did McKernan crack his helmet.

"Let's get going."

They drove for a couple of hours, pretty much in silence, Ortiz taking the first stint. It was just before dawn when they got started, but the constable could drive in the tracks they had made on the way there, so they made decent time even before the sun came up and they could see their surroundings clearly.

McKernan dug some breakfast bars out of the food locker and mixed up some powdered juice. He went to where Philips sat in the back.

"Hungry?"

At first Philips was indifferent, but it had been at least ten hours since he had eaten. He took the offered bar and cup of juice and ate hungrily.

When he was done, he handed the cup back to McKernan and asked, "What's going to happen to me?"

"To tell the truth, I'm not sure. This isn't a situation we have to deal with much. I'll take you back to Mars City with me and turn you over there when I file my report. I expect they'll ship you back to Earth and deal with it there. There aren't any prisons on Mars. No courts or lawyers, for that matter."

"I don't want to go back to Earth," Philips said with resignation.

"You should have thought about that before you killed Augustyn."

Philips just shook his head.

They drove through the morning, McKernan taking a shift to relieve Ortiz. They were making good time, but it would still be after sunset before they got back to Station Alpha. Philips continued to sit silently in the rear of the buggy. McKernan was starting to worry about his prisoner, afraid that he might become suicidal. The most obvious ways might take Ortiz and him with him.

He decided that they should take a brief break for lunch hoping that he might be able to break the prisoner's mood. Philips ate the offered cup of soup readily enough, but still remained silent unless addressed directly.

Ortiz took the driving shift after lunch. McKernan kept an eye on the prisoner.

"Look," McKernan said finally, "you're going to have to make a statement sooner or later. We really don't have anything to do for the next six hours. You might as well make it now. The buggy is equipped with a recorder. Is that okay with you?"

"Whatever you want," Philips replied. "I guess it doesn't really matter."

"Okay, then. Might as well get started," he hit the recording control on the console."

"Please state your name, age, date and place of birth, and occupation," McKernan said formally.

"Jason Philips, 33 years, March 17, 2065, Los Angeles, California. I am, I was the maintenance technician at Research Station Alpha."

"Did you kill Dr. James Augustyn?"

"Yes."

"Why did you kill him?"

"He had found out that I had been arrested for selling drugs as a kid. He said that he was going to turn the information over to the Trust Authority. That would have meant that I'd be sent back to Earth. I didn't want that. There's no place for me back on Earth. I wouldn't be able to get a job."

"Was Augustyn blackmailing you?"

"Blackmailing me," Philips said puzzledly. "I don't have any money. Don't really need it here."

"Did he try to make you do anything?"

"Yeah. He wanted my help. He wanted me to alter some of the data Boris Federenko had been collecting. Wanted to make it look like he had been faking his research. I refused. Boris always treated me okay. I think Dr. Augustyn wanted to discredit him so he could sleep with Dr. Toranaga. When I wouldn't help him he said he'd get me. That's when he found out about my arrest and said that he'd turn the information over."

"Nice," Ortiz commented from the driver's seat.

"I don't think we need editorial comments, constable," McKernan said. Not that he didn't feel the same way.

"Anyway, he said he was going to get me sent back to Earth. That's when I decided to kill him. Is that all you need?"

"Not quite," McKernan responded. "I need you to go through the night of the murder step by step. When you killed Dr. Augustyn, how you got past the security, where you got the hammer, what Augustyn was doing? All the details. Why don't you start with when and how you got into the lab."

"Is this really necessary? I've admitted that I killed him. Isn't that enough?"

"I'm afraid we have to go through it. I've got a report that I have to file. You know how paperwork is."

"Yeah, I guess so," Philips agreed grudgingly.

"So what time did you enter the lab?"

"It was about 03:30. I waited until everybody else had gone to bed. Some of the scientists had stayed up playing cards late, so I couldn't do it earlier. I waited until I could hear Dr. Chen snoring. I got up and went to the lab."

"How did you get into the lab without triggering the lock alarms and keeping the computer from registering the lock cycling?"

Philips thought about that for a moment.

"I'd rigged a code into the computer. It was something that I used for maintenance, so I could work on the lock without disturbing anyone. It's against regulations, but techs do it all the time."

"So you were able to open the lock without having the alarm sound?"

"Yes. All I had to do was enter the code. That kept the lock from registering on the computer, too."

"What happened next?"

"I went through into the lab. I could see Dr. Augustyn in his office. He was working on something late. He did that a lot. I think he was working on something he didn't want anyone to see."

"Did he see you?"

"Yeah, I think so. His office is right by the airlock. I don't think he could have missed me."

"Wouldn't he think it strange that the lock alarm hadn't sounded?"

"Maybe. I don't know. He didn't pay a lot of attention to how things worked."

"What did you do next?"

"I went back into my workroom. It's towards the other end of the lab building."

"Why did you go there?"

"That's where the hammer was. There's a lot of surplus equipment back there. Stuff that's been left by people when they go back to Earth. I thought if I just grab one of the hammers laying around, no one would trace it to me. I also got a disposable coverall and put it on. The kind that I use if I have to work on the reactor."

"So you got the hammer. What next?"

"I went back to Dr. Augustyn's office. He was at his desk working on his computer, but he heard me and turned around. He saw the hammer in my hand. I think he realized

I was going to kill him because I could see the fear in his eyes. I swung the hammer at his head and hit him. The blood splattered everywhere. That's why I wore the coverall. I hit him a couple of more times to make sure he was dead. Then I left."

"What did you do with the hammer?"

"I left it buried in his head. I could see his eyes still open."

"What did you do after that?"

"I went back to the workroom and took off the coverall and put it in the disposal unit. I washed my hands and face to make sure there wasn't any sign of blood. Then I went back out through the airlock turning off the maintenance code. Then I went to bed."

"What time was this?"

"I don't know. It must have been 04:30. It really didn't take very long."

"What happened in the morning?"

"I slept until about 07:00. I got up and went to breakfast. While I was eating Dr. MacKensie came out of the lab and said Dr. Augustyn was dead. He told me to put a lock on the door so no one could get in until you arrived."

"Did you look inside the office at that time?"

"No. After Molly had a look at the body through the door to confirm that he was dead, Dr. MacKensie closed it. I was getting the lock and some tools while that happened. I never looked into the office."

"So you couldn't say if the body or the hammer had been disturbed after you left the lab?"

"No, but why would it have been. And the only person who had been in the office was Dr. MacKensie. He made sure of that."

During most of the statement Philips had been quiet and assured, but now he seemed to be getting nervous.

"Is there anything else that you want to add?"

"No. I don't think so."

"And you attest that everything you have said in this statement is the truth?"

"Yes, I do."

"Statement of Jason Philips taken at 14:00 by Inspector Erik McKernan and witnessed by Constable Elena Ortiz." He hit the control to stop the recording. As he did so, Ortiz gave him a quizzical look. McKernan suspected that the constable, like him, had found at least a few things in the prisoner's statement that didn't match the evidence from the crime scene.

Ortiz had been over the computer code of the airlock alarm system. There had been no evidence of any sort of maintenance "trapdoor" code. As to the hammer, Dr. MacKensie had stated that it had been laying on a shelf in Augustyn's office for days before the murder. But the most important difference was that Augustyn had been hit only once from behind, not repeatedly from the front. Either Philips had lied in the statement, or he had never seen the body at all. Either way, he wasn't telling the truth, but the question was why.

He had a lot of time to think about it. Philips had curled up on the bench in the rear of the buggy. He could see that Ortiz had as many questions as he did, but wasn't going to raise them in the presence of the prisoner.

They traded driving shifts after that, McKernan driving into the late afternoon before Ortiz took over again. By the time they reached Station Alpha, they were driving by headlights but the track had been easy enough to follow.

McKernan unshackled the prisoner and gave him back his helmet. He went through the buggy's lock first. Philips followed, and then Ortiz. They used the same order with the station lock.

"What are we going to do with him, Inspector?" Ortiz asked.

"We'll be going back to Junction 3 in the morning, Philips. If you give me your word that you won't try to run away again I'll let you go to your quarters. If not, I'll have to shackle you to your bed. It's you choice."

"I won't run away again, Inspector," Philips answered.

"Good. I'm going to take your surface suit and lock it up, just in case." Philips handed over his helmet and then unzipped his suit, handing it over when he was done. He pulled a coverall from his locker and headed to the administration building lock.

After he was gone, Ortiz looked at McKernan. "He didn't kill Augustyn, did he?"

"No, I don't think so. But I think I know who did."

Ortiz looked at her superior, but he wasn't ready to say anything more.

"Let's see if we can get some dinner," McKernan said, after they had finished stowing their gear.

They cycled though the lock to the administration building. Molly was still in the kitchen cleaning up after dinner.

"I thought you might still be hungry so I made some sandwiches and left some soup on the burner. Grab a table and I'll bring it out."

The four card players were still at it, so they picked a small table off to the side of the room where they could talk without being overheard. Molly came out a few moments later with a tray. She set it down on the table saying, "I can see you two have something to talk over. I let you alone," before she returned to the kitchen.

After three days of living in their surface suits and driving they were both hungry and tired. Real food had never tasted so good, but it only took them a few minutes to finish.

"So are you going to tell me?" Ortiz asked finally as she sipped her coffee.

"Not just yet. I think I know who killed Augustyn. I just don't have any proof. And I'm not going to make an accusation without having something more to go on."

"But Philips didn't do it," Ortiz said.

"No, that confession he gave us was so full of holes that I think we can be sure he's the one person that didn't kill Augustyn. He never saw the body or the wound. We know the hammer that was used was sitting on the shelf, and not one from the stores. And there's absolutely no evidence that the lock records or alarms were tampered with."

"So why did he confess?"

"He's trying to protect someone. He figures that his past is going to come out no matter what happens and he'll be sent back to Earth. For him that's as bad as a prison sentence. He's got nothing to lose by confessing. The question is, who is he trying to protect? And is he doing it because he knows who killed Augustyn, or because he thinks he knows who killed Augustyn?"

"But you must have some idea?"

"Figure it out for yourself, Constable."

"What do you mean?"

"What are the three things they tell you to look at when investigating a crime? Motive, means, and opportunity. Well, we've already established that everybody here had some sort of motive."

"Everybody except for Dr. MacKensie," Ortiz commented. "But most of them don't have a strong motive."

"At least that we know about," McKernan responded. "As to means, the hammer was sitting on the shelf right by the door. Anyone entering the office could have grabbed it as they walked through the door. And these are all fit people. Anyone of them could have swung that hammer with enough force to smash in Augustyn's head.

"So where does that leave us? Opportunity, that's where. And that's where the evidence is weak. We don't know exactly when Augustyn was killed. All we know is that it was sometime between 24:12 and 07:30 the next morning. It could have been 24:13 or it could have been 07:29 any time in between. And that makes a big difference. At 03:00 everybody is supposedly snug in their beds, or at least someone's bed.   At 07:00 some people were already up and moving about."

"But we don't know when he was killed," Ortiz said. "We didn't get to the scene until two days after he crime and the body had been sitting undisturbed all that time in a room with the heat turned off. No way to determine the time of death. Dr. MacKensie did the right thing securing the crime, but it's too bad he didn't at least let Molly or someone feel the body when he discovered it to see if it was still warm."

"Yes, too bad. Of course, there was no need to see if Augustyn was dead. That was pretty obvious. But it still would have been helpful to have the one trained medical professional, Molly who is a nurse, give at least a cursory examination of the corpse. Of course, Dr. MacKensie was just securing the crime scene, as you said, and you can't fault him for that."

"What?   Do you think he was trying to protect someone? Who? Philips?"

"Think about it, Constable. Dr. Augustyn enters the empty lab wing at 24:12, presumably still alive. At 07:30 when Dr. MacKensie comes out of the lab to announce the crime, Augustyn is dead."

Ortiz's eyes got wide as the realization struck her.

CHAPTER 24
DAY 6, 22:00-23:00

McKernan noticed that the light was on in MacKensie's office. As he passed the door, he glanced in and saw the station chief sitting at his desk, a bottle of Scotch next to him.

"Care to join me in a drink, Inspector?"

"Don't mind if I do," McKernan replied entering the office and taking a seat in the other chair. MacKensie reached into a desk drawer and pulled out another glass pouring three fingers of the amber liquid. The Scotch was the real deal, not a local product, single malt, 12 years old, Speyside.

MacKensie, noting the inspector's raised eyebrows said, "One of the perks of being head of the station. A friend of mine on Earth packs it in along with supplies for the station. Good Scotch is one of the few things I miss about not being on Earth."

McKernan took a sip of his drink. It always surprised him how smooth it could be while still burning.

"You've been on Mars about what, Inspector? Six years?" MacKensie asked.

"About that?" McKernan replied.

"Are you going to stay?"

"I'm thinking about it?"

"Let me give you a piece of advice. If you have any doubts at all, don't leave it too long. Six years is about the limit. Longer than that and you won't fit in on Earth anymore."

"That has occurred to me," McKernan said. "I'm not sure that I'd fit in now. About the only job I'd be qualified for would be U.N. commissioner for some failed state or other."

"Don't sell yourself short, Eric. You don't mind if I call you Eric, do you?"

"You're the man with the good Scotch. So are you recommending I go back to Earth?"

"No. Mars needs good men. Men like you. I'm just saying that you should be sure before you commit yourself. There is a point of no return. I found that out the hard way."

The two men sat there for a while savoring their drinks before MacKensie asked, "How is your investigation going?"

"I think it's just about finished. Ortiz and I will be leaving tomorrow."

"What's going to happen to Jason?" MacKensie asked.

"I'm not sure. As far as I'm concerned all he's really done is borrowed a buggy for a joy ride. That's a matter between him and the station."

"You don't think he is the one that killed James, then? I'm relieved to hear that."

"I thought you would be."

"So you've determined who killed James?"

"I think we both know who did it," McKernan said.

The station chief sighed and took another sip.

"How long have you known?"

"I've had my suspicions from the start, but I've really only been sure for the last few hours, when I decided Jason couldn't have done it."

"I see, what gave the murderer away?"

"I kept trying to find a way past the security on the airlocks between the buildings. It was pretty straight forward. You left the lab building around midnight just before Augustyn entered. At that time he was the only one in the lab. There were four witnesses that can corroborate all of this. The security logs don't show any activity until you entered the lab building at 07:30 the next morning. Unless there was some way out of one of the other buildings and into the lab without setting an alarm, there was really only one possibility. Ortiz and I have checked everything, there just isn't any way to bypass the airlock alarms. That left only one possibility, you killed Augustyn after you entered the lab in the morning."

"I see. And you're sure of that?"

"Yes. You killed him, immediately had the door locked so no one could check the body and had Jason turn down the temperature to preserve the corpse. You knew that it would take at least a half day for anyone to get here from Junction 3, longer if they came from Mars City. You contacted Garcia-Gomez to make sure that I would be sent to investigate. That made it nearly a day and a half before anyone checked the body. By then the body would be cold and it would be difficult to determine when the time of death was. All we had was your statement that Augustyn had been dead for some time when you discovered it."

"As they say, your logic is impeccable."

The two men sat there in silence looking at each other.

"Your glass is empty, inspector. Care for another? It seems a shame to let this Scotch go to waste."

"I don't mind if I do." MacKensie poured another couple of fingers in each of their glasses.

"You know of course what Augustyn had been doing?" the station head asked.

"That he had been blackmailing several of the staff and trying to force his attentions on Toranaga? Yes I knew about that. Also that he had something on Jason Phillips and was threatening to have him sent back to Earth. I discovered some microfilmed documents that he had hidden in his office. I admit that he was not a very ethical individual, doctor."

"No he wasn't. I could stand by, Eric, when he tried his tricks on the staff. I knew that they could take care of themselves, at least with a little help from a friend. But you know, James, in the position he was going to get as head of the Planetary Institute when he went back to Earth, would end up in control of Station Alpha. Technically, the station operates under the aegis of the Institute. I couldn't accept that, of course. A man like that running all the research on Mars. I had tried to stop his appointment, but James was too well connected politically. At least now, that won't happen."

"I think it was Jason, though, that put me over the edge. He's been on Mars or the Moon longer than you have, inspector, nearly eight Earth years without being back. I know what it would be like if he had to go back. It would cut years off his life, maybe kill him outright. And he'd never be able to get any sort of decent job. He's too good a man for that. That's what I went into James' office to talk about, try to persuade him to change his mind about going to the Trust Authority with the information on Jason. He just ignored me. He said that he had a duty to perform and the matter was settled. Then he just turned his back on me. A man's life in the balance and he just turned his back on me. That was what did it. I saw the hammer sitting on the shelf next to the door. I picked it up and struck. It didn't take much. There wasn't even much of a mess. He was dead instantly."

"I shut the door, and then called Jason to put a lock on it so no one could get in until you came. Then I put in the call to Garcia-Gomez."

"You know I could understand Jason's plight. The last time I was on Earth I couldn't stand it more than the few weeks it took to arrange a return flight. The doctors told me then that I'd die if I ever came back to Earth. I'd spent too much time on Mars. My heart couldn't take the higher gravity. Jason has been off Earth nearly as long."

"I discovered a few months ago, Eric, that I have cancer. It's a kind that can be treated—on Earth. The facilities on Mars just aren't up to it. So I can go back to Earth and die of heart failure or stay on Mars and die of cancer in the next year or so. There really wasn't any choice for me. I've come to love this planet. I have from the first time I set foot on the surface twenty five years ago. I think that's why I couldn't let a worm like Augustyn muck it up with his petty games."

He took another sip of his Scotch.

"So what happens now, Inspector?"

"Ortiz and I are leaving in the morning, We'll take Augustyn's body with us. I'm afraid that you'll have to come along as well."

"And the information James had on people? What happens to that?"

"I don't see that it has any bearing on the case. I see no need to put it in my report."

"Thank you, Inspector. I hope you do choose to remain on Mars."

He took a last sip of his whisky and stared at the bottle. Shaking his head, he replaced the stopper and handed the bottle to McKernan. "You might as well keep this."

"Am I under arrest?" MacKensie asked.

"Where are you going to go?," McKernan answered. "I'm sure that you have some things that you need to settle up. Arrangements to make for handing over control of the station to one of the staff. I'll leave you to it."

McKernan drained his drink and stood up.

"And Dr. MacKensie, thanks for the Scotch. I appreciated it."

He left the office and went through the airlock to the administration building.

CHAPTER 25
DAY 7, 07:00-08:30

McKernan was having a cup of coffee in the dining room while he waited for Ortiz. It was very good coffee, at least by Mars standards, the real thing from Earth. Good coffee massed the same as bad, and transportation costs far outweighed the original price on Earth. The scientists at Station Alpha did enjoy their little perks.

When Ortiz showed up she was still wearing her surface suit, sans helmet.

"Phillips helped me stow the body on the buggy. We're ready to go when you are."

"Good, we can leave as soon as we finish breakfast. By the way, Doctor MacKensie will be joining us for the trip."

Ortiz gave him a questioning look but said nothing.

The sun was just coming up giving them a spectacular view out the dining room windows. Despite the danger of that much exposed glass, McKernan could understand why the station had been designed as it had.

"Did you talk with MacKensie?" Ortiz asked as she sipped her coffee.

"Last night. He confirmed everything. That's why he will be joining us on our trip back."

"Where is he now?"

"You don't have to worry. He's not going to escape. There's no place for him to run to. Besides, the doctor is an honorable man. But to answer your question, I think he went outside to view one last sunrise."

"Is that wise, sir? In his state of mind."

"I think it's for the best. We owe him this last look. Mars owes him."

They sat in silence eating their breakfast of eggs, pancakes and sausage links. The other residents of Station Alpha had started to file in for breakfast. The weather had finally cleared and they were all eager to get out and do some field work.

Suddenly they heard a chair scraping as it was pushed back from one of the tables and a stifled "My God."

David Chen approached them and said, "Inspector, I think something's wrong. I was watching Doctor MacKensie looking at the sunrise and he just collapsed and is laying there."

McKernan stepped to the window and looked where Chen was pointing. A man in a surface suit was lying on the ground.

"You'd better get out there Ortiz and see if there's anything you can do. I'll join you as soon as I can get my surface suit on."

It was five minutes later when he joined her as she stood over the body. They were at the very rim of the cliff on which the Station sat and the ground dropped down a hundred meters before them.

"He's dead, sir. There must have been a problem with his carbon dioxide scrubber. He passed out when the CO_2 level got too high. I don't understand. There should have been an alarm sounding in his suit. He would have had time to get to the air lock."

"There must have been a malfunction," McKernan stated flatly. "We'll have to take the suit and the body with us in the Mars buggy, so that they can be checked at Mars City."

After he had helped Ortiz with the body he reentered the station. Everyone had gathered in the lounge area, where they had been looking out the window at the spot where MacKensie had died.

"Ladies and gentlemen, there's been a tragic accident. Doctor MacKensie is dead. It appears that there was a malfunction with the carbon dioxide scrubbers on his suit. He lost consciousness before he could get back to the airlock. He may not even have been aware that there was a problem."

"That's impossible," Nils Jensen cried. "Mac was a fanatic on safety. He always double checked everything and kept his equipment in top condition."

"Nevertheless, he's dead," McKernan said. "Mars is a dangerous place that can kill even the most careful of us. I'm very sorry about this. I liked Dr. MacKensie. He was a great man who loved this planet. He'll certainly be missed. Of course, there will be a full investigation. Constable Ortiz and I will be taking the body back with us so that they can be examined at Mars City."

"Yes, of course," Jensen responded.

"Inspector," Chen interrupted, "what about the murder? Have you figured out who killed Augustyn?"

"I've completed my investigation and come to the conclusion that it was not a murder but a case of suicide. There is no way anyone could have entered the lab building from the time Dr. Augustyn entered until Dr. MacKensie discovered the body in the morning, and the whereabouts of all of the station personnel has been accounted for during that time period. Dr. Augustyn was the only person in the lab building at the time his death occurred. Therefore, it must have been a suicide."

"We're supposed to believe that he killed himself with a hammer blow to the head? Is that even possible? I know Augustyn was an unfeeling bastard, but if he was going to kill himself there had to have been an easier way."

"As Holmes once said, Dr. Chen, when all other possibilities are ruled out, the remaining one, however improbable must be the truth. We have four witnesses to his entering the empty lab building. No one else entered until Dr. MacKensie in the morning when he discovered the body. You certainly don't think that Dr. MacKensie killed him, do you?"

"No, of course not," Chen replied. "Oh--."

"I think you will all agree, ladies and gentlemen, that a great enough tragedy has occurred this morning, without tarnishing Dr. MacKensie's reputation with idle speculation. You are all aware of Dr. Augustyn's shortcomings as a person. I think that we can safely say that remorse over those shortcomings led directly to his death and leave it at that."

There were a lot of sideways glances between the various occupants of the room, but no one saw fit to speak up.

"If there are no further questions, Constable Ortiz and I have a long journey to Junction 3 and need to be on our way. I'm sorry things turned out the way they did, and hopefully the next time we meet will be a happier occasion. Constable."

The two left the lounge and headed towards the airlock.

EPILOG

Several days after Chief Inspector McKernan returned to Mars City the Interim Trust Authority Governor signed off on his report on the deaths at Station Alpha. The death of James Augustyn was ruled a suicide by means of a self inflicted wound. The death of Dr. William MacKensie was ruled an accident due to an equipment malfunction.

Dr. MacKensie had no close relatives either on Mars or Earth. In accordance to his wishes as expressed in his will his body was returned to Station Alpha for burial. There was a simple ceremony at which the Interim Trust Authority Governor Hugo Garcia-Gomez and Chief Inspector Eric McKernan and a number of other officials were present as well as all of the staff of Station Alpha. Only the limitation of transport prevented a larger attendance. A live video feed of the ceremony was beamed around the planet and was viewed by many of the long time residents of Mars. It was said that a moment of silence was observed by those that had gathered at Finnegan's.

The body was buried on the edge of the escarpment close to the spot where he died. It was placed so that he could watch the sun rise over the plain. A small marker was later placed over the grave bearing the inscription:

WILLIAM MACKENSIE
He Gave His Life to Mars

The escarpment was later renamed the MacKensie Escarpment and Station Alpha is now the William MacKensie Research Station.

THE END

SPECIAL PREVIEW!

THE BLOOD RED SANDS OF MARS

By Greg Fowlkes

Book One from the Murder on Mars Series

Now available from The Fictional Press
www.TheFictionalPress.com

THE BLOOD RED
SANDS OF MARS

The wind was blowing again against the west wall of the hut. He could hear the grains of sand abrading the thin aluminum skin that protected him from the outside. Through the window, half frosted from the continuous onslaught of sand and dust, he could see clouds of dust obscuring the sky. The sky was a pastel pink, a color no sky had any right to be. The wind, despite its 120 kph. velocity, made only a thin howl as it blew over the half buried cylinder of the hut.

McKernan lay on his cot trying not to admit that he was awake. It was a losing battle. After a few minutes he surrendered and glanced over at the clock sitting on the crate next to his bed. The dim red digits of the LED display read 7:58. It was too early to get up, too late to go back to sleep. He rolled over, shivering at the cold. The temperature couldn't have been more than ten degrees Celsius inside the hut. For the twentieth time he thought to himself that he would have to fix the heater before winter— if he could get the parts. Either that, or put in more insulation—if he could find that. The cold finally forced the decision to get up.

Standing, he felt the cold plastic floor beneath his bare feet. With his foot he fished the worn and patched pants from beneath the cot and pulled them on. He dug underneath his pillow and came up with a switchblade knife that he stuck in his pocket before drawing on the turtleneck sweater that had lain next to his pants. The cold feel of the cloth did nothing to dispel the cold from his body. From the crate he picked up a shoulder holster with a small automatic pistol and put it on. McKernan drew the weapon, worked the slide once, and after examining it perfunctorily, placed it back in the holster. Satisfied, he pulled on a worn pair of leather boots and placed another knife in a sheathe between his skin and the boot top.

Dressed, he went over to the shelf that served as counter and table. He put a pan of beans onto the heating unit and got a soysteak from the small refrigerator that held up one end of the shelf. The steak went into the frying pan on the other heating element. An egg would have been nice, but at the current price of three dollars apiece it was an extravagance that he would have to put off for a while.

As the food cooked he drew a liter of water from the spigot in the corner of the hut and watered the plants in the garden under the window. The carrots and tomatoes were doing nicely. He smiled briefly because it would be good to have fresh vegetables for a change. The big, leafy oxygen plants were doing well, too. He would be able to cut down on his oxygen ration this month and save some money.

He took the beans off the heating element and replaced them with the coffee pot. The beans were still half cold, but he wasn't in the mood to hassle with them. He only had the two heating elements, and he didn't want to have to wait for his coffee. He forced down the beans and then wolfed down the steak. It almost tasted like real beef, but then maybe his memories were fading. As usual, the coffee tasted terrible and tepid, too. The air pressure in the hut was too low for water to boil properly.

He finished his meal and scraped the remnants of food into the pressure vessel that served as a compost heap. The gauge on its neighbor showed that he had almost half a tank of methane. He'd be able to sell that soon and use the money for something useful, like a still. Completing his rounds, the gauges on the life support systems showed that everything was still working at keeping him alive. He went back to the pots and scrubbed them clean with sand. That, at least, was plentiful and cheap.

He checked his watch against the clock. It was time to get going. Pulling on his jacket he went to the airlock at the corridor end of the hut. After checking the gauge to make sure that there was pressure on the other side, he undogged the latches and stepped through. Closing the door behind him, he repeated the process with the outer hatch, latching both doors behind him. The outer door he locked with a heavy padlock.

He had entered a low tubular corridor made of the same aluminum foil and plastic foam construction as the hut. The walls, however, were even thinner, and no pretense was made of heating it. He could see his breath condensing in front of him as he began to walk down its length. It was a hell of a way to live, he reflected, not for the first time. But then, it had been hell living in L.A. where he'd been born, with brown air, rats, a chronic shortage of water, and overcrowded tenements. He had made his choice, but sometimes it seemed as though life was a continual shiver.

The corridor was pierced at regular intervals by hatches identical to his own. The huts behind the hatches were identical, too, except for the modifications the owners had made to make them more livable. This part of the city was old, dating back a couple of decades to the first days of the settlement when it had been part of a scientific base. The scientists had departed, at least from that corridor, and been replaced by those who had the money to buy or rent the huts from the Trust Authority. Maintenance was pretty much left up to the residents.

Along the sides and overhead ran the pipes and conduits that pumped in the gases, liquids, and power necessary for sustaining life. The whole system looked as jury rigged and fragile as it actually was, though surprisingly few people died whenever the system failed. Martians were a cautious lot. One didn't talk much about injuries. Accidents on Mars didn't leave many.

A hundred meters down the tube he came to an airlock. Going through the same ritual that he had used on his front door, he went through to another length of corridor indistinguishable from the one he had just left. Continuing on, he passed through two more airlocks until he entered a corridor that sloped downward. The hatches were farther apart, and larger. Signs overhead indicated the businesses or functions that were carried out behind them. The air was warmer because the corridor was buried beneath the sand which provided insulation. At the end of the tunnel was a larger airlock set into a wall of fused silica bricks, the first substantial piece of construction he had met that morning.

Passing through the portal was like entering another world, which in a way he had. This was the public Mars, the planet seen by the corporation men and the officials of the Trust Authority. It was also the planet seen by tourists, the brave new colony, man's first outpost on another planet. The tourists didn't really care to see the hut town. They were part of the same world as the corporation men and the government types. It still took a great deal of money or power to reach Mars.

The difference was more than one of degree. For one thing, the temperature was a comfortable twenty. For another, the walls were flat and met the floors and ceilings at right angles, unlike the inflated skins of the huts and corridors. With a little imagination it could almost be an enclosed shopping mall on earth, though the presence of fused silica blocks was more prevalent than any architect would allow.

The most important difference, however, was the sight of people scurrying along. He hadn't met anyone in the outer corridors. People rarely lingered there because of the cold. Now, McKernan could see at least twenty people and it was still fairly early. No airlocks interrupted this corridor. Extending for two hundred meters in either direction, it was twenty meters wide and ten high, the largest enclosed volume on the planet. Arrayed along its length were the offices and store fronts of the corporations that owned Mars, as well as the more prosperous saloons and bordellos.

One day the Trust Authority promised that the whole city would be like that, with apartments and condominiums for the ordinary workers, but neither the Authority or the corporations had yet come up with the money. For the moment all that existed was the one street of a few blocks.

McKernan headed towards the Authority's offices which dominated one end of the mall, but turned aside at the last moment when he noticed that a small, dark doorway was open. He knew that he should resist the temptation, but he was not in a very disciplined mood. He went through the doorway into the darkness beyond.

Finnegan's was the only real, honest bar on Mars. There were any number of saloons and even a cocktail lounge in the Mars Sheraton, but only one quiet, dark place where a man could drink in peace. McKernan felt the need for some of that peace at the moment.

He sat down on one of the stools before the only mahogany bar on Mars. Finnegan, himself, was behind the bar, though in fact he almost always was, no matter what the hour.   The bartender looked up and greeted the newcomer, "Good morning, constable. Beer or whiskey?"

"It's too early for beer. It's too early for whiskey, but give me a shot, anyway."

Finnegan poured out a shot glass of amber liquid and placed it before McKernan and then stood back polishing a glass while he studied the man opposite him.

McKernan knocked back half the glass before he spoke. When he did, there was a bitter edge to his voice. "Sometimes I wonder if it's worth it, Finnegan. I could be back on a planet fit for human life."

"Could you, now, constable?" Finnegan said, putting down the glass and picking up another in equally gleaming condition. "If mother earth was such a bed of roses, why are you here?"

He breathed on the glass and examined it against the light for a moment, then looked at McKernan with the same intentness. "You're here because you're not the sort to live off the dole or to spend your life with another man being your boss. Instead you'll spend your life trying to make this planet a fit place to live and retire in twenty years with a nice pension. Now drink up and get to work, laddy."

"Yeah, sure. Sorry to burden you with my problems. Early morning depression, I guess. See you." He finished off the shot and left five dollars in Authority script on the bar.

The bite of the whiskey so early in the morning didn't really help his disposition, but it did give him enough courage to make it to the office. The morning ritual at Finnegan's was becoming too much of a habit. His three years on Mars were beginning to show.

The jail wasn't in the brick part of the Authority building, but in the complex of pneumatic architecture that sprawled behind it. The huts were old—older than his own—but dated back to the days when governments had not begrudged a few billions for exploration, back before space had to show a profit. For that reason, they were sound and well insulated, though a bit tacky looking.

The jail consisted of two huts joined together, one for offices, the other for the two makeshift cells and storage. Ferris was the only one there when he walked in, a young kid, younger than he had been himself when he had come to Mars. He was still impressed enough with his responsibilities and had not yet been worn down by the grim realities to take his job in any way but seriously.

Ferris greeted him with a solemn, "Good morning, sir," with a stress on the sir. As a three year veteran of Mars, Ferris looked on his boss with more than a touch of awe.

"Anything exciting happen overnight?" McKernan didn't really expect much. A few fights in the saloon district, a knifing maybe if things got out of hand. Petty thievery, or perhaps not so petty. He looked at Ferris and saw a flash of excitement in his eyes that the younger man was trying hard to suppress in order to match the hard bitten image he had of his superior.

"Yes, sir. We've got a murder on our hands."

"Another knifing down at Thelma's?" he asked, naming an infamous saloon and bordello that figured in a quarter of all the police reports.

"No. A prospector was found out on his claim yesterday, over on the far side of Olympus Mons. He was shot, Inspector."

That was bad, McKernan thought. People on Mars weren't supposed to have guns. With the thin skins of most buildings and a hostile atmosphere outside that would support life exactly as long as you could hold your breath, they were dangerous, and not just to the targets. The Authority had made them illegal and the corporations had been more than willing to agree. They weren't easy to get—not something that could be picked up casually or made, like a knife. Even without the details it sounded like the work of a real criminal and not just a squabble over a claim or a woman.

"Okay. Let me have the report. I'll take a look at it."

He took the folder from Ferris who looked a bit crestfallen. *He probably expects me to go rush off to the outside and track down the murderer like an Indian scout,* McKernan thought. *He'd learn in time.* Mars was a big planet and a dangerous one, but because of its nature there were also very few places that a man could run to and none where he could hide indefinitely.

He was leafing through the report when he came to his door. For the thousandth time he read, "Inspector Erik McKernan, Chief Constable." *Mother would have been proud,* he thought sardonically. She had hated the L.A. cops like all the other residents of the barrio. He went through the door into the little cubicle that was his real home. There, sitting at his desk, he began to read the report, sketchy though it was, to look for some explanations.

THE FICTIONAL DETECTIVE
BY GREG FOWLKES

WHO KILLED EZEKIAL O. HANDLER?

A beautiful dame, a hard-boiled private eye --- and a dead body.

It started like any other case. When a famous writer dies in a mysterious car crash, private detective Frank Slade is called in to find answers, but all he finds is more questions. Who killed Ezekial Handler? Who is Janet Nielsen and why is she so interested in finding out? Who is leaving the neatly typed clues? And as Slade tries to find answers to these questions he starts to wonder if the ultimate answer will threaten his very existence.

Now available from The Fictional Press.
Buy it on Amazon.com!

THE LAWS OF MAGIC
BY GREG FOWLKES

Egil Njalson was an aspiring lawyer. A lawyer with a difference. Not only had he passed the bar, but he had an undergraduate degree from the most prestigious school of magic in the country, the California Institute of Thaumaturgy. Needless to say his caseload and clients tended to the unusual. Like witches; or vampires. And the opposition, well they were likely to be demons. But Egil Njalson had sworn an oath to uphold the law of the land, and...

THE LAWS OF MAGIC

Now available from The Fictional Press.
Buy it on Amazon.com!

The Fictional Press
www.TheFictionalPress.com

About The Fictional Press

The Fictional Press, an imprint of Intrepid Ink, LLC, provides full publishing services to authors of fiction and non-fiction books, eBooks and websites. From editing to formatting, to publishing, to marketing, Intrepid Ink gets your creative works into the hands of the people who want to read them.

Find out more at www.thefictionalpress.com.

www.ingramcontent.com/pod-product-compliance
Lightning Source LLC
Chambersburg PA
CBHW070924180626
46817CB00003B/1187